COASTAL CONSPIRACY

COASTAL ADVENTURE SERIES 1

DON RICH

Library of Congress PCN Data

Rich, Don

Coastal Conspiracy/Don Rich

A Coastal Adventure Series Novel

Florida Refugee Press LLC

Cover by: Cover2Book.com

This is a work of fiction. Names, characters, and incidents are either the product of the author's imagination or are used fictitiously. Any resemblance to actual persons, living or dead, businesses, companies, events, or locales is purely coincidental. That being said, the overall familiarity with boats and water found in this book comes from the author having spent years on, under, and beside them.

Published by FLORIDA REFUGEE PRESS, LLC, 2019

Crozet, VA

FOREWORD

The idea of nicknames for most if not all of the dockside characters in this book might seem farfetched and overdone, but it's not. Back in my teens and early twenties I "worked the boats." If you were given a nickname it meant acceptance into this close-knit fishing community that was comprised of some real characters. Some were from as far North as Nova Scotia, and as far South as Key West, plus all points in between. We all had these things in common: a love of fishing, the water, and of boats. Oh, and beer. Beer ranked right up there.

The Beer-Thirty-Bunch was based on a group of guys that I used to hang with after four-thirty (we didn't knock off early, our days started before most folks in office jobs even thought about going to work.) It was this strong sense of community that went beyond the dock and out on the water with all of us. We shared fishing information over the radio, often in our own code. Back at the dock, we told each other stories of nightmarish boat owners who fortunately were few and far between. Often job offers were ignored or declined based on what was common but quietly shared knowledge gained back at the dock. We looked out for each other, on land as well as on the water.

Craziness after hours was totally acceptable (well...mostly) and often made "Caddyshack" look like a Disney film. What else would you expect from a group that participated in the annual "Mullet Gutter Open?" This was a golf tournament where baseball bats were often used as drivers, pool cues as putters, and where we ran the beer cart ragged. Off-season dock parties were common, too. There was a time during one of them when a live shark ended up in the old Sailfish Marina pool.

So, trust me that Baloney and his pals aren't too far off from "the norm." I had a ball fishing with and learning boat maintenance from their predecessors. It was here that I also gained my great appreciation of boats and the water. Thanks, guys.

To those who have "crossed the bar" before me: Hap, Little Pete Jeff, Splittails Charley, Betterway, and the rest. Also, to those who still go to sea in boats: Chris, Nolan, Rufus, Rusty, Jay, and Mike.

PROLOGUE

2:00 am Mallard Cove Marina, Southern Tip of the Eastern Shore of VA

THE DARK BLUE 110-foot steel research vessel *Robert E Grisham* pulled slowly into the smaller eastern basin of the marina complex. This was the commercial side and usually, only a few older boats were moored there. Lately, the *Grisham* had been the sole tenant along the wharf side, something which pleased Captain Altan Kamal. The fewer eyes around to see her late-night comings and goings, the better.

At first glance, the *Grisham* looked like so many other aging research vessels of her size and vintage. She featured a high bow with a raised and enclosed bridge deck forward, and a huge seventy-five-foot long by twenty-six foot wide open main deck aft. The only thing which looked slightly out of the ordinary was that instead of a more common "A" frame gantry crane at her stern, she had a large deck-mounted boom crane. Other than that, she looked like the dozens of her sister ships that could be found in ports all over the world. She was dented and battered and ringed with almost two dozen truck tires down each side. These tires were attached to the hull with large, rusty chains, and they served as fenders between the *Grisham* and the concrete seawall.

Her almost fifty-year-old hull was quickly reaching the end of its lifespan, as the maintenance the *Grisham* received had been minimal at best over the last decade. Because of this, her owner had been able to purchase her for next to nothing a couple of years ago. Her 1692 Detroit diesel engines were almost run out, and the increasing groaning noises during rough seas as her steel plates flexed and moved were becoming a big concern to Altan. Because of her age and advanced wear, the *Grisham*'s next stop would likely be some breaking yard to be recycled, rather than a shipyard for a refit. Fortunately, most of the trips she took these days were short, and most of her other time was now spent alongside the wharf. Her decrepit looks also meant that almost no one would give her a second glance at any commercial port, which was also a big part of the plan.

After Altan's cousin Volkan attached the *Grisham*'s mooring lines to the bollards on the concrete bulkhead, he climbed the deck ladder up to the bridge. In their native Turkish language, Volkan told Altan he would call their patron and report that the transfer went well, and the container was now onboard. Patron was the Turkish word for boss, and theirs was a man they both feared. The man, known to them only as "the American," was the one who, through an offshore shell corporation, owned the *Grisham*. The patron had devised and founded the business they were engaged in and had the connections to dispose of their cargo. He had also designed the specialized forty-foot containers that the business required. It was one of those containers the cousins had just transferred from an incoming freighter to the deck of the *Grisham*, almost twenty miles offshore.

From the exterior, the container looked like any of the millions spread around the globe. Its markings showed that it was owned by a fictitious company and that it was a forty-foot "Reefer" or refrigerated unit. A heavy cord snaked from it over to a connection under the port bulkhead. If you listened closely, you could hear a small cooling unit running at the front. But instead of the normal ultra-high fan-forced air, the output from this one was similar in temperature, volume, and noise to a large wall-mounted air conditioner. The unit allowed fresh air to be exchanged without any noise from the inside being overheard outside.

The interior of the container was set up as a mobile dormitory with a dozen bunk beds, and a primitive bathroom. Plywood walls covered the sprayed urethane foam insulation which provided both temperature protection as well as sound deadening qualities.

The American sounded pleased with Volkan's call. "Good. Then we will be on schedule to load and ship this first group from here. We have room for two more in this shipment though."

"Elif and I will find two more before then." Volkan sounded confident. Elif was his sister and hunting partner, and she was very good at her job.

"Make sure they are blondes or redheads; they bring a higher price. Our Arab customers prefer those."

"We will do our best, patron."

"And remember to be very careful not to lead anyone back to the farmhouse. It cost me a small fortune to have to switch bases from New Jersey because of that last fiasco you created. I hope I don't need to remind you what is riding on this."

"No, patron. We will be extra careful."

The American grunted and hung up. Volkan shuddered, recalling that a cousin of his had disappeared back in Turkey thanks to the American, who had a long reach. The patron said he had wanted to teach him a lesson, and that was why his cousin was now gone. This was because back in New Jersey, Volkan had gotten sloppy and disobeyed the American's order to never return to the same place to hunt for the next girl. But hunting on the boardwalk in the little New Jersey town had seemed so easy. He hadn't figured on there being so many undercover police around.

Volkan and Elif had barely gotten away in the swap car before the police had a description of it and then issued a BOLO alert for them. They had just enough time to torch the old staging place and flee before it was surrounded. Fortunately, they had already shipped all but one girl, and they took her with them.

The American had developed a backup plan just in case something like this were to happen. He had already been planning to move the operation to Virginia in the next year but hadn't yet told any of the crew. And their cousin's disappearance wasn't at the behest of the American though he led them to believe it was. The timing was just too perfect and having them fear him even more had a huge benefit. Though he knew not to turn his back to either one of them.

Having the *Grisham* now berthed at Mallard Cove was the result of over a year of research and planning by the American. From here she would have a much shorter run to meet the incoming and outgoing freighters bound to and from ports along the Chesapeake. He actually couldn't believe his luck when he stumbled onto it. The place had very little traffic, deep water, easy wharf side access for vehicles, and a short run to the sea. The crumbling marina ensured that there would be fewer and fewer boats and people around. Plus, its proximity to the rented farm that became their staging place meant less exposure on the road for the containers and their valuable cargo after they were pre-loaded there.

The Shore was the last place the police would think to look for girls taken from places with larger populations like Richmond, Charlottesville, Virginia Beach, Hampton, Annapolis, and Delaware. The roads leading from these places were large, crowded, and had multiple lanes. Not great candidates for roadblocks when they were fleeing from the site of a snatch job. He couldn't have been happier with how it had all worked out. Now they were ready to ship their first load of young girls to the Middle East from this new location. All of his planning was paying off.

1

OLD FRIENDS

Michael "Murph" Murphy emerged from the salon of his vintage forty-seven-foot Rybovich sport fisherman, *Irish Luck,* just as the sun peeked above the horizon. He could already feel it was going to be another warm and muggy end-of-summer day. A laughing gull yelled at him from atop a piling in the empty neighboring slip as he sipped his first cup of coffee and settled into the cockpit's fighting chair. He didn't have any charters booked until the weekend, and since this was only Wednesday, he could afford to relax.

Basically, there are two types of sportfishing boats, private ones, and ones that charter. Of the ones who charter, those that focus on the "tourist trade" are built to stand up to a lot of rough traffic. Their decks are usually gel coated or painted to stand up against non-rubber-soled shoes. And there's also no fancy varnished trim to be found onboard. Others like *Irish Luck* do run private charters, and their clientele expects a higher level of finish and comfort and are willing to pay for it. Their decks are oiled teak, and there are copious amounts of varnished wood everywhere. Translated, it means these boats are maintenance nightmares. However, they command a much higher rate from their clients who show up in deck shoes rather than leather-soled street shoes and cowboy boots.

Usually, these boats aren't booked as often as their tourist trade counterparts, and their charters happen through client referrals. This ensures that their clients aren't people who would be rough on either the boats or the crews because word of that would get around fast in this close-knit community. Murph looked forward to this weekend's charter; a nice family he'd known from around the docks down in Palm Beach. They had gotten wind he had gone into business for himself, and that the white marlin are thick off Virginia right now. He wanted to put them on as many as possible and hopefully cultivate their repeat business.

A minute later two arms wrapped around Murph's neck. A mane of blond hair spilled down over his left shoulder and someone wrapped him up in a head-turning kiss.

"Good morning, babe!" Lindsay Davis, his twenty-six-year-old girlfriend, first mate, and now business partner reached across and stole his coffee mug.

"Hey! Get your own."

"It's brewing. And I thought we were partners."

"Business, yes. Coffee, no. Give it back!"

She reached down and released the swivel lock on the chair's base and gave the varnished teak slat seatback a shove, sending Murph spinning around to face her. She climbed up across his lap with a mischievous grin, holding the mug out beyond his reach. "Come get it!"

"Are we still talking about the coffee, Linds?" Murph now matched her, grin for grin, as he wrapped his arms around her.

"For an old guy, you sure are frisky."

"OLD? I'm only thirty-five! And since when did you start complaining?"

"We both know parts of you are older and have much higher mileage." She loved teasing him about his past reputation for having been a "player" back in his native Florida. "And no, I'm not complaining." She snuggled up against him.

"Good, because we have the day off, and can go log more 'rack time.'" His grin got wider.

"Sorry, babe, remember I'm headed up to go shopping with Dawn today."

Murph scowled, partly out of disappointment, and also because Dawn was his ex-fiancée who was now engaged to his old friend, real estate investor Casey Shaw. Casey had also been his long-time boss and short-lived business partner. Murph seemed to have forgotten that he caused both breakups. He had gotten involved with Lindsay during a rough period between him and Dawn.

Lindsay hadn't known that he wasn't unattached at the time, and broke things off as soon as she found out. What followed were months of Murph hounding her until she finally forgave him. And as much as he was glad that she had made a friend since her move to the Shore and their moving in together, the fact it was Dawn worried him. How it had come about could best be described as complicated. It happened while Murph and Casey re-bonded at an alcohol-fueled, post-fishing tournament celebration.

"Kind of creepy, you now hanging out with Dawn."

Lindsay's smile became even more mischievous. "Why? Are you afraid that she's going to share some deep, dark, secret about you?"

"No, it just gives me the creeps, that's all."

"Well, we get along great. We enjoy each other's company and have sooo much in common." Her eyes danced as she ribbed him. "Besides, since you and Casey are back to occasionally spending time together, why shouldn't we? If it weren't for the two of them, you and I would never have won the Presidential White Marlin Tournament, and that two-million-dollar first prize. And there would be no way we could be even considering buying *Mallard Cove* without it." An angler on Casey and Dawn's team had noticed something that helped prove another crew had cheated, moving Murph and Lindsay up into first place. It was the richest tournament on the East Coast.

"And speaking of that, maybe I should see if Casey has time for lunch today. We could talk about that restaurant deal, and you and I can ride up together. Unless you want me to wait until you can be there, too."

"I think it would be a good idea for the two of you to meet first. Depending on what happens, I can always join you when Dawn and I get back."

Lindsay and Murph had recently signed a contract to purchase the *Mallard Cove Marina* property. It was the only commercial property at the southern tip of the Eastern Shore of Virginia, also known as ESVA. The marina was situated between the Atlantic Ocean and the Chesapeake Bay, on the southern border of the Eastern Shore National Wildlife Refuge. It was the first property you passed when exiting the Chesapeake Bay Bridge-Tunnel (CBBT). For the last forty years, it had been owned by an older curmudgeon named Voorhees who had run it on a shoestring. As he had approached retirement age, he had stopped all spending on repairs and maintenance, mostly because he wanted to pull out more cash as a nest egg. But it was also because the business had declined as the place fell into disrepair, leaving less available cash. He finally decided to sell and approached Murph and Lindsay to see if they had any interest in buying him out. He knew Murph had been involved in real estate and that the pair had some recent tournament winnings. The truth was that most of Murph's real estate involvement had been as Casey's "right-hand man" in Florida, maintaining his commercial properties as well as his boats for fifteen years. While he had learned a lot during that decade and a half, his first venture in real estate had only come about when he moved up to Virginia's Eastern Shore with Casey. He had been his original partner in the now highly successful *Chesapeake Bayside Resort* project, but Casey had ended up having to buy him out.

The old wood docks in the big western basin at *Mallard Cove* had once held well over a hundred boats. But many of the pilings had now rotted to the point of not being trustworthy enough to even hold a rowboat in a stiff breeze. Plus, when it had been constructed, the average fishing boat was much shorter and narrower, so even the "good" slips couldn't fit the larger more modern charter boats. The property also had an old restaurant with an attached ramshackle office that had been shared with the dockmaster, back when there used to be one on-site. The building sat in between the marina and the CBBT, but the restaurant had been closed for years. However, the screened-in patio dining area which overlooked the marina still hosted afternoon beer drinkers from the marina's boat crews in a "bring your own beer" kind of way.

Murph and Lindsay had brought *Irish Luck* to *Mallard Cove* right after he bought her, back when money had been tight. The slip rents were cheap, and from here they had easy access to both the Atlantic and the Chesapeake. The vintage Rybovich sport fisherman had been built about the same time as the marina, so she fits one of the remaining usable slips perfectly. They planned to do more tournament fishing, and book longer trip charters. With those longer high-end private charters, they generally picked up their fishing parties at other locations. So, it didn't matter that they were based out of such a crumbling place.

The "Rybo," as the brand was nicknamed, had more of a yacht finish and feel to it than the typical mid-Atlantic charter boat. Her varnished aft bulkhead, double teak flybridge handrails, and varnished teak toe rails on the bow, along with oiled teak decks and covering boards gave her a very elegant yet classic look and feel. And the word was spreading about their recent successes at two of the biggest mid-Atlantic tournaments, which had given a big boost to their bookings. They weren't planning on snagging the spontaneous tourist business from off the docks, so they could've cared less about *Mallard Cove*'s current appearance.

Immediately east of the big basin was the smaller but deeper one which held a few commercial boats including the research vessel *Robert E. Grisham*. On the North side there was also a large "ways," an old drydock mechanism built right after World War II. Two metal railroad tracks were mounted on what looked like a wide concrete boat ramp. The rails held a steel-wheeled angled wooden platform that dropped back into the water like a huge boat trailer, pulling out boats for repair. It was hauled back up by a thick and rusty cable, attached to a mechanism powered by an ancient Ford "Model A" engine. It was an old way of doing things, though there were many smaller ones still operating on the Shore. Most newer boatyards used mobile strap lifts, which were faster and more versatile, but expensive to purchase. Beyond the ways were several scrub-covered acres that had been originally intended to be incorporated into the boatyard. But the mobile railway system which would have attached to the ways for moving drydocked vessels had never been built by Voorhees, leaving the land to become overgrown.

Murph and Lindsay quickly recognized what a great opportunity it was to be able to purchase this property. They also understood the locals would view them as outsiders, which was a huge hurdle down the road if they wanted to get approval for building more than what was already there. There might be a chance to do something with the extra acreage at some point, but that would depend on a blessing by the local politicians. Meanwhile, they would need a lot of cash just to reconfigure and renovate the marina and the restaurant. However, they weren't interested in running a restaurant; they only wanted to rent slips and sell gas, beer, and ice. They figured it would be easy to find a new dockmaster, and they could rent out the restaurant. This was what Murph had suggested to Casey, and what he wanted to follow up on with him now. They would need the income because they had stretched financially to buy the property. And, even by doing it in phases, the initial marina renovation would delete most of their current cash reserves. The good thing though was they wouldn't have any personal debt, something that both he and Lindsay wanted to avoid.

Murph wriggled his cell phone out of his pocket without dislodging Lindsay and he started to text.

"Oh, that's your phone! I thought it was too big to be..."

"Very funny. Gimme a minute."

She looked at the screen. "Isn't it too early to text him?"

"Unless it's the weekend, he's always up and working before dawn. Most of the time with Dawn, too." He sent the message as Lindsay got up to go check on her coffee. She came back a few minutes later with a full cup for each of them and reclaimed her seat on his lap. Murph had already turned the chair back to face the dock.

"Casey's up for getting together. He was about to text me and suggest it. We're having lunch at the *Bluffs*, their new marina on the ocean side. I haven't seen that yet, they bought it after I left. I think he wants me to see what they've done with that restaurant. This is a good sign he's interested and wants to make a deal."

A pair of loud diesel engines interrupted Murph as they cranked up two slips over. This was followed by the stench from a cloud of black smoke caused by two sets of worn-out injectors. A minute later Captain Bill Cooper, better known on the docks and at the afternoon "Beer–Thirty–Bunch" as "Baloney" appeared behind *Irish Luck*.

"Hey! Can I come aboard?"

Murph answered, "I dunno, can you? Aren't you afraid the *Golden Dolphin* will run off and leave you?"

Bill hopped onto the aft covering board and down into the cockpit, leaning back against the transom. A colorful character in his early fifties, he was balding, with gray temples, and stood just under five feet, six inches tall. Though his big, booming, heavily New Jersey accented voice almost made him seem taller. He already had his first cigar of the day clamped between his teeth, though by his wife's rules it was never lit until he passed through the breakwater.

"Good morning, Lindsay." He beamed at her as so many men did. "And no, my mate Bobby knows better, Murph. Haven't seen nary a sign of our charter yet, but these guys always run late, so I wanted ta warm the engines up and be ready ta cast off, soon as they show. So, is it true?"

Murph looked puzzled. "Is what true?"

"Scuttlebutt has it you two are buying the place."

"We have a contract on it, but we haven't closed yet."

"You're not going to turn it inta one of those mega yacht marinas and kick us all out, are ya?"

"Not on your life. But we are going to fix things up a bit." Murph smiled.

Lindsay jumped in, "Bill, there's no way we want you going

anywhere! You and the *Golden Dolphin* are a fixture around here, and we want it to stay that way." She smiled as Bill looked relieved.

"And you're not raising my rent?"

Lindsay shook her head. "We don't have any plans to anytime soon."

Murph added, "But we will need your cooperation when we start work on the slips. May need to get you to move down a few slips, but only temporarily."

"I can still go back ta my corner slip, right? I've had that spot for over ten years, an' I'm the first charter boat they see coming in from the road. You can see Santa up there from over on the road." Every year before Christmas, Cooper put a life-sized Santa dummy with a beer can in his hand up in his tuna tower with a floodlight trained on him. It was kind of tradition, just as his hanging a black brassiere from his starboard outrigger line was whenever they caught a wahoo.

Lindsay said, "Your spot is safe. Don't give it another thought."

"Thanks, you guys. That's a load off my mind. Nice ta know the place'll still be here, an' I'll be here with it."

"Trust us. We're going to fix things up and see if we can't draw in a few more customers for you. New fuel pumps and tanks, too." Murph gave him a reassuring nod.

"Oh, hey, here's my charter. I gotta go."

As Bill hopped back up to the dock Lindsay called out, "Catch 'em up, Cap!"

He bellowed back over his shoulder in his boat voice, "It's what I do best!' Addressing his charter, he bellowed, "Hey, grab yer gear and get aboard, the cobia are hittin' hard and we're burnin' daylight!"

Lindsay chuckled. "He's wasting his money on a VHF radio. I think they can hear him all the way over at Virginia Beach without one."

Murph laughed. "Yep, he's got about the same range. If you can see him, you can hear him."

They still heard him even over his diesels as he issued orders from his flybridge and idled out past the breakwater. The aging yellow wooden hull of the *Golden Dolphin* disappeared in a cloud of black smoke as he throttled up his old engines.

"Now, was all that smoke from his engines or his cigar?" Lindsay laughed as she said it, and Murph joined in.

"Probably both. I'm glad he plans on sticking around, he adds a lot of life to the place."

"Volume, too."

A LITTLE OVER an hour later the pair were headed North on 13 in Murph's pickup truck. Murph hadn't said a word since they left *Mallard Cove*, fifteen minutes ago.

"Everything all right, babe?"

"Yeah, I'm just thinking."

"About?" Lindsay looked concerned.

"It's a little weird. I started out on my own when I got Casey's old boat *Migration* in that settlement from my last bosses' estate after they died. Those idiots almost got me killed by being cheap." Russian gangsters had murdered his bosses in a case of mistaken identity; they had refused to change the name of Casey's old Hatteras because of the cost involved. The gangsters had been after Casey and Dawn but ended up holding Murph hostage. They had cut off his right pinky finger during the ensuing ordeal.

"Then I sold *Migration* and bought *Irish Luck*. Casey finally bought back those property shares he had given me as a bonus, and now we're kind of doing what he set out to do when we came up here. At least the marina part. It seems like my path keeps getting wrapped up with his, or like I'm copying him."

"But you might say his path, or his life is kind of paralleling yours too since he's with Dawn now. He copied you!" She grinned.

Murph looked thoughtful and he nodded. "Maybe a bit, yeah."

"Besides, this isn't only your life, it's *our* life. Our business. Together. No longer about you alone anymore, pal. So, what if we are copying what they've done? I don't want to reinvent the wheel. I want a safe business that's throwing off cash and growing in value while we're off fishing together. Let someone else blaze the trail, let's do whatever allows us to do the other things that we love doing.

"We know the price we are paying for the property is low for what it is, and where it is. We also know we can grow the marina business once we get the docks fixed up. Having income from the restaurant property without the hassle of running it will be great."

"I only hope I can talk Casey into leasing it."

"Says the man who hounded and hounded me after I no longer wanted anything to do with him. Babe, you can talk anyone into anything when you want to. Trust me on that!"

It was Murph's turn to grin as he glanced over at her. "Thanks for the vote of confidence. I'll do my best."

She reached over and massaged his shoulder. "You always do."

LINDSAY'S EYES grew wide as they drove through the gate at *Bayside*. "Wow! This entrance turned out gorgeous. The landscaping is amazing! The last time I went down this driveway, it was all still gravel and weeds."

The drive was now asphalt and lined with cold hearty palms and large, sculpted planter beds filled with flowers and mulch. A manicured grass strip filled the area between the beds and the driveway. To their right, another driveway with electric gates had been installed. This appeared to lead to a section of new mini-estates. Murph drove several hundred yards until he came to a three-way fork. Straight ahead lay the marina and beach café parking lot. To the left was a driveway with a security fence and another electric gate. Beyond it, on the South dock, *Lady Dawn* was tied up out by the inlet. This 110-foot Hargrave yacht was Casey and Dawn's home.

And even though most of their business was transient, the marina was still over half-full in the middle of the week despite this now being past the peak season. To the far right, a circular drive led to the portico of the hotel. Across the circle at their near right was a new long, low and unassuming single-story building with parking in front and back. It contained the offices of McAlister and Shaw as well as

ESVA Security, a firm owned by Rikki Jenkins and her partners. She was also a good friend and fishing partner of Casey and Dawn.

"This was so rundown a year ago, and that building wasn't here."

Murph agreed, "You're right, Linds. Welcome to the world of how fast Casey Shaw can move. I gotta admit though, this even blows *me* away. It came out great."

They parked and went through the glass doors into the reception area. The walls had numerous aerial photos of the property, and artist renditions of the *Bayside Club and Spa* buildings that were now under construction. Dawn emerged from a long hallway. At five-feet, eleven-inches tall with a fantastic figure, bright blue eyes you could see from across any room, and long flowing red hair, she was a stunning thirty-year-old woman.

"Lindsay! I'm so excited to take a day off and spend it with you."

"Me too, Dawn. I've been looking forward to a girl's day."

"Uh, hi, Dawn?" Murph shifted uneasily from foot to foot.

"Hello, Murph." The temperature in the room suddenly dropped a few degrees.

He looked at her hopefully. "You think you'll ever be up for the whole 'forgive and forget' thing at some point?"

"Put it this way, Murph. I haven't pulled a gun on you yet today so that's a start. But the day *is* young so don't push it." She cracked an evil-looking grin.

"Good morning!" Casey came into the room and gave Lindsay a light hug. "I understand you two are going to do some retail therapy today."

She beamed at Casey. "I'll try not to get Dawn into too much trouble."

Casey's large golden retriever bounded up to Murph, giving him a "play bow" and sitting at his feet while holding up a paw and letting out a big "Woof." Murph took the paw with a huge grin and said, "Hello to you, too, Bimini!"

The two had spent almost as much time together over Bimini's lifetime as he had with Casey. He rolled over on his back for a belly rub as Murph squatted down to oblige him. Then a very attractive, long black-haired young woman in her mid-twenties came into the room. Murph's eyes locked on her, scanning from toes to nose, something not lost on Lindsay. Casey made introductions.

"Lindsay, Murph, this is Kari Albury. Kari works closely with Dawn and me on the *Bayside Estates and Club* project, and I've asked her to join us today. As a native, she's got a lot of ESVA knowledge, and she also has a natural knack for understanding real estate."

She blushed at the compliment. "Thanks, Casey, but I'm just learning. It's so nice to meet you both, Dawn has told me a lot about you two." She looked straight at Murph, her eyes narrowed, and silently screamed, '*Back off, bucko!*'

Casey looked at Dawn, "Are you sure you don't want to stay for our meeting?"

She eyed Murph then looked back at Casey. "Positive!" Then she hooked her arm through Lindsay's and led her down the hallway toward the back parking area.

Casey looked sheepish after Dawn's comment. "Well, okay then. I know it's been a while since you've been here, Murph, so would you like to see what we've done with the *Bayside Dining Room* and the *Rooftops Bar & Grill*?"

"Sure, yeah. Maybe see what you might want to do at *Mallard Cove*."

Casey and Kari exchanged glances then he said, "We also want you to see what we've created over at our *Bluffs Restaurant and Marina*. Carlos is over there today, showing the crew some new menu items and I know he'll want to say hi to you. He's running our culinary division now that has these two restaurants, plus the *Bayside Beach Café* and the *Bluffs Restaurant*, and he's designing two new venues at the *Bayside Club*, plus another at the *Spa*. We're also building a new bakery that will supply all the venues with fresh baked goods. We made Carlos a partner in the restaurants with us."

Casey and Murph had brought Carlos Ramirez up with them from Florida. They recognized his natural culinary talent that was being wasted working as a fry cook in a marina restaurant there. They had seen a glimpse of his abilities which had then blossomed at

Bayside. An unexpected bonus was that he turned out to be a great restaurant designer and logistician. Casey and Dawn had made him a restaurant partner partly to ensure he wouldn't ever leave *Bayside*. His food was already drawing rave reviews in many regional magazines.

Murph said, "I'm really glad for him. He took quite a chance coming up here with us."

"Yes, and he's thrilled with the challenges we've heaped on him." Casey mentally kicked himself for saying that because he knew that a big part of why Murph left was that Casey had pushed him too far, too fast, "overloading his plate." He didn't want Murph drawing comparisons and getting his ego bruised. He was in for enough surprises today as it was, and Casey wanted him in a really positive mood.

The three of them walked over to the hotel and left Bimini back at the office as they checked out both restaurants. The last time Murph had been here they had been in the process of interior demolition, so he was really impressed with how well each had turned out. The *Bayside Dining Room* was a more formal venue, with some marina views through the windows. Directly above was the *Rooftops Restaurant*, with the same large footprint. That space was roofed and screened on three sides. It overlooked the marina and out toward the Chesapeake Bay and the view was incredible. Back in the far corner against a brick wall was an open charcoal grill with a kitchen behind one end of a long bar. The grill had become known for its house-aged steaks and grilled fresh seafood.

Murph knew that Casey was a wizard at renovating commercial properties, but this was a whole different ballgame, and it was obvious he had let Carlos lead the design. He liked what he saw and was really looking forward to checking out the *Bluffs*. It sounded like it was very similar to *Mallard Cove*, with an older marina and a new restaurant.

They went back to the office where Murph got to meet Cindy Crenshaw, another of the partners in *Bayside*. She was in charge of operations for the company and was also the reason that Casey and Dawn didn't need to spend every waking hour on-site.

Casey, Kari, and Murph loaded into Casey's old Jeep Cherokee for the ten-minute ride to the *Bluffs*.

"I like the new ride, Case!" Murph wasn't being sarcastic. While the Jeep was over ten years old, Casey had just purchased it. This was one of the vintage, squarer models. One of the ones with all the aerodynamics of a brick.

"My last one started having issues, and I found this one online. Less than 20,000 miles, garage kept and in mint condition. You know how I love these."

"Yeah, I do. Nice ride. In the fifteen years I've known you, I've seen you go from an old ratty thirty-one-foot Bertram to that Hargrave, but you've never had any other model of car. Nice to know that some things never change."

Casey looked over at his old friend and nodded. He was glad they had gotten past their differences and were spending time together again. He had really missed that.

2

MAKING PLANS

"Wow, Case, another nice entrance." Murph liked the almost tropical feel of the pampas grasses, cold weather hardy palms, and broad leafed plants that lined the long driveway. "Feels a bit like Florida in ESVA."

"That's what we were going for. We wanted it to look a bit different, and it worked; our customers like what we've done. Plus, we didn't want to go in direct competition with existing local restaurants by offering the same food choices. We didn't go at it intending to put other folks out of business, and I think we've gotten that point across. We didn't make any friends, but more importantly, we didn't make any real enemies, either."

They pulled up to the parking area in front of the huge Seminole Indian built thatched roof chickee that covered the screened outside seating area. It was attached to what appeared to have been an older house, one of three that stood side by side on the property. They all faced the water. Casey led them around back to the cantilevered open deck that overlooked the marina. It was at the bottom of the hill, set back into the grassy mud flats. Beyond that was a channel that led North and South that separated them from the scrub and dune-covered barrier islands beyond.

"Kind of reminds me of the marina restaurant back in Riviera Beach, Florida, where you kept *Migration*."

Casey nodded. "It does. Only here, we let Carlos use his imagination with the menu. And speak of the devil!"

"Murph! It's great to see you, man!" Carlos emerged from the chickee and hugged his friend.

"You look great, Carlos. This place must agree with you."

"It does. I'm so happy here with what we are doing. And Casey tells me we might get a chance to work together again."

"We're talking about it, yeah. And I've been Jonesing for some Carlos cuisine!"

"Well, I'll fix you right up just like I used to. Hey, I've got to get back inside, I'm introducing the crew to some new menu items. But I wanted to come out and say hello first."

As Carlos disappeared back inside, Murph turned his attention to the marina basin where the same crew that had rebuilt *Bayside*'s docks was at work on the far side. "What's going on over there?"

Kari had been quietly standing in the background listening, but now she stepped up, holding a rolled plan she had brought with them and spread it out on a table. "We're maximizing the number of slips. When this was built, they only installed the one dock on our left, and only extended it as they filled the slips and needed more space. We're going ahead and building the maximum number of slips that we can fit, using prefabbed concrete and foam floating dock sections. While it's not as aesthetically pleasing or eco-friendly as the recycled materials used at *Bayside*, the idea here was to get the most bang for our buck, like with the food. Same great quality, but more of a standard fare at lower prices, targeting a different segment of the market. We're going to promote the *Bluffs* next year by hosting a couple of tournaments and believe me, we'll fill this place after people see it."

Murph looked over the plans then back at Kari and nodded. "Nice. I like the floating docks, especially for boats that have absentee owners. No worrying about adjusting lines during storms or spring tides."

"Exactly." She looked pleased. "Plus, we're adding marina cams on our website so you can check on your boat anytime you want from your home or office. More peace of mind."

Casey said, "Let's take a tour of the interior, and show you how we converted the house." He took them through, showing off the new commercial kitchen where Carlos was holding court with the *Bluffs'* kitchen staff, then the main dining room which was decorated with numerous photos that showed off the natural beauty of ESVA. Some were taken from the air, some from the water, and others from the land.

Out in the chickee, the water view was the biggest feature, followed by fishing mementos of Casey's, including trophies from recent tournaments in Virginia Beach, and Delaware. They picked a table away from the door with a good view of the docks and where they could see the bow of Casey's fifty-five-foot Jarrett Bay sport fisherman, *Predator*, sticking out beyond a few neighboring boats.

Their waitress came over and took their drink orders, telling them that Carlos had already picked out some new menu items for them. Kari sat back and listened intently to Murph and Casey's conversation, as she had been doing all morning.

"Seems like old times back in Florida, Case, with Carlos trying out new menu items on us." Murph smiled widely as he recalled the memory.

Casey nodded. "Kari, Carlos worked at this little fry joint at the marina where I lived. He kept wanting to add new items, but the owner wouldn't hear of it. So, Carlos would play around secretly in the kitchen, and sneak us stuff that he created off the menu. The owner didn't understand how talented Carlos really was. The sad part was that he didn't even care. So, it ended up costing him Carlos, as well as who knows how many thousands and thousands of dollars in missed sales. All that he could have had simply by empowering him and encouraging his talent. Remind me to send him a *Thank You* card." He chuckled and shook his head.

Kari nodded and smiled. She was picking up a lot of knowledge from Casey, and it was part of why she loved working with him. His sense of humor was also part of it.

"So, Murph, why another marina, and why now?" Casey leaned back to listen and gave Kari a glance, silently urging her to do the same.

"Case, you always said that a property could 'talk' to you, and this one screamed at me." He paused and grinned before continuing. "It's rundown, has deep water access, lots of acreage with commercial zoning, and most importantly, it's the first thing you see when you hit ESVA. The current owner only sees it for what it is, not what it could be. So, it was easy to get him to agree to a reasonable price."

Casey chuckled, "Kari, to translate from 'Murph-ese' that means he stole it."

Murph grinned. "He made a wise choice by accepting a very reasonable counteroffer."

Casey rolled his eyes. "Make that, he *really* stole it." Kari stifled a laugh.

"Case, down the road this place could be worth a fortune. They're building the first of the parallel tunnels in the Chesapeake Bay Bridge-Tunnel system and in a few years when the second one is built, it'll eliminate the bottlenecks and allow double the amount of traffic that can come across at peak periods. The tourists are coming, Case, and they'll see my docks and restaurant first."

"So, you and Lindsay are looking to get out of the charter business?" Casey wanted to drill down on Murph's line of thinking.

"No. We will still charter and tournament fish, but we can hire someone to rent the slips, and sell the fuel, beer, and ice. That's why we don't want the headache of a restaurant, we only want the rental income from the building."

"How much of a note are you taking out?"

"We're not taking out a loan, we're paying with all the cash from our tournament winnings. We'll have just about enough left over to put in new fuel pumps and tanks plus replace a few of the slips. And we'll do the rest as we can out of profits."

"That could take a long time."

"Business will pick up as we fix things." Murph looked hopeful, wanting Casey's approval of his assessment.

"So, your long-term goal is to make your money by selling the appreciated property, and in the meantime maybe have it throw off a little cash."

"Exactly!"

Casey looked at Kari. "You want to bring in your laptop?"

"Sure. Be right back."

As she went to the Jeep, Casey looked back at Murph. "I'm going to tell you exactly what I'm thinking and don't get mad. Dawn and I talked it over, and we don't want to lease your restaurant. At first, we thought we'd offer to buy it from you, but I got Kari to look at the whole property, and I'll let her show you what she came up with. Having no personally guaranteed debt is a good thing, without a doubt. But putting that much money into the project and having such a small return until you eventually can sell the property is not your best option, in my opinion. That's a ton of cash out of pocket, and you really aren't adding value, you're only going back to maintaining it properly. It's not the highest and best use of the land. You're on the right track, but you are missing some huge points."

Kari came back and opened a large screen laptop on the table in front of Murph. Casey said, "You want to take it from here?"

She nodded. "Thanks, Casey. Murph, you were right in tying up this property thinking there would be good future value. But I think you are overlooking a lot of hidden value that already exists which could throw off a ton of cash." She started a slideshow of photos of various features of the property.

Murph was already upset over what he felt was a turn down by his friend, and now some girl he didn't even know was now apparently going to lecture him on his project. "Hey! Where did you get those pictures?"

"I went down there and took them myself the other day when you were out on a charter. Casey asked me to look into this after you'd mentioned it to him, and I'm glad I did. When you identify the property boundaries, you'll find there's so much more property there than it appears at first glance. The longer you wait to put it into use, the more income you'll be missing." She brought up an aerial shot with the actual property lines inserted. "Modernizing the docks would be great, and fixing up the old restaurant would help, but you are paying for all this land that's just sitting there doing nothing and costing you in taxes. It needs to pay for itself, as well as do something to help you fill those slips. But sitting vacant, or worse, continuing to get overtaken by weeds and scrub will do nothing but detract from the improvements you are going to make to the marina."

Murph nodded curtly as he processed her points. But she did have his full attention.

"So, I did a little research as to what would be the highest and best use for that parcel. While there are some new hotels and motels a few miles north on US 13, there isn't anything new directly on the water. Also, there's no in and out interior boat storage with multi-level racking anywhere around that can accommodate today's longer and wider outboards. Here's my suggested best use for the property." She switched to a site plan showing an in-and-out boat storage building at the end where the commercial basin was. Opposite the other basin was a multi-story zig-zag-shaped building with a huge pool that faced the marina and the water beyond it. A new restaurant was between the hotel and boat storage building with a glass-enclosed bar overlooking the marina basin. The existing restaurant now sported a deck that overlooked the marina. A sand volleyball court had been added out by the small beach. She then paged through more artist renderings of what each building would look like.

Kari saw that she now had his full attention. "Murph, this way we get them to come and stay for a few days. Once they are here, they're more likely to go on a fishing charter and hang by the pool or the adjacent bar. The in and out storage over here to the east is a perfect complement to the hotel. Not many outboards have cabins. Say someone hasn't yet reached the point of affording a bigger boat or only wants a center console style. Say they work in Virginia Beach, Hampton, Norfolk, or Richmond and want to get out of the city for the weekend. They book a hotel room and then call to have their boat pulled out, launched, and fueled up so it's ready to go when they get here. It's the perfect getaway place for someone who can't yet afford *Bayside* but wants to be treated like they can. Impresses the hell out of their friends.

"Okay, that part will be repeat business from spring through summer. Then we have the diehard rockfish, or like they call them if they're from out of state, striper fishermen. We're the closest hotel and marina to the CBBT, also known as big rockfish central in November and December. The slow months will be January through March, just like they are for everyone else on ESVA. We make our money the other nine months."

Murph was taken aback. "We?"

Casey smiled. "Now you see why I wanted Kari to join us today. She's good, isn't she?" Kari smiled back at Casey, then looked at Murph.

Murph wasn't smiling. "What is this 'we' stuff? You don't want to lease the restaurant, so you're out. And I don't have the cash to do all this." He gestured toward the laptop.

Casey put his hand on his friend's arm. "When I bought your *Bayside* shares back, remember how I stretched the payments out over three years? Do you know why I did that?"

"Yeah. To help your cash flow." Murph scowled.

Casey shook his head. "No, I could have easily paid you in one lump sum. Stretching them out like that was to help protect you from yourself. I wanted to be sure that you would still have some income while you built your charter business. I was afraid that if I paid you upfront, you might do something reckless with it. Like putting all of it into one deal, just as you plan on doing on this property with all of your tournament money.

"We've been friends for a long time, Murph. I've never pulled any punches with you, and I'm not about to start. It may seem like it's a safe bet to dump all your cash into one piece of property to avoid debt, but it's not smart. Yes, that property is a great investment, but only if you have enough cash to make the improvements and build an income stream from it right away. The slip rent will barely cover the insurance and the taxes. Running that property this way is like owning a race car but without having any money for gas. And what happens if you blow one of those old Cummins engines in your Rybo, do you have the cash to replace it? You'll have to sell a lot of beer, gas, and ice to pay for one of those."

"So, what now, you want to buy me out of this deal too Casey?" Murph said angrily.

"I didn't want to buy you out of the first one! You were the one who wanted out. You left, remember?"

"And you tried to screw me when I did. What you offered me was a joke!"

"Murph, if you remember, I *gave* you those shares in the first place. You never laid out a dime for them."

"And I gave you a decade and a half of loyalty, honesty, and hard work for them. When it was just you and me working together Casey, we were fine! I didn't want to quit working for you, I just wanted to get the hell away from that leech of a second wife that you married. I didn't pull any punches with you, either. You know now I was right about her, but you couldn't see it until it was too late, and it's going to cost you a ton of cash in your divorce. I sure as hell could see it was bound to happen and I told you that, but you wouldn't listen to me."

Both men had leaned forward across the table as the argument got more heated. Kari leaned back in her chair, trying to decide if she should get up and leave to give them their space. But she decided she should stay alongside Casey instead. If he hadn't wanted her there, he would have already said so.

Murph continued. "That was probably the best thing that ever happened to me. It forced me to go out on my own and make my own decisions. That's what I've been doing ever since, and I've been doing great. I sold your old boat for more than you did and bought that Rybovich for a song. Now I've tied up the best piece of available property on the Shore, all by myself. Why do I need you?"

Casey leaned back and regained his composure. He looked straight into Murph's eyes as he answered quietly. "For the same reason that I needed Dave. He had more experience than I did, and I ran over every deal with him. Dave never pulled any punches with me either, and there were many times that I didn't want to admit I was wrong. He helped me see when I was. But you know this because you were there for a lot of it. He kept me from taking a wrong turn. I learned from him because he'd already made the same mistakes."

Murph leaned back too, and his features softened. He knew how hard it was for Casey to talk about Dave. He had been Casey's best friend and mentor as well as the best man at Casey's wedding, just a week before he and his wife were murdered a year ago. Dave had meant the world to Casey and had always watched out for him since he was sixteen years old. Almost two decades older than Casey, he had given him his start in real estate and partnered with him on several deals. Mostly though, he had been a father figure to Casey.

Both men had been orphans who had bounced around within "the system" as kids, and each started out on their own when they were barely old enough to drive. With similar backgrounds, the two had formed a bond tighter than many fathers and sons. Both ended up making fortunes in real estate in South Florida and living aboard their boats in the same marina. But Casey wanted out of the congested rat race it had become and made the move up to Virginia. It had been difficult to leave Dave behind, but he hadn't regretted the move.

Murph was about to tell Casey he was wrong when his phone rang with Lindsay's ring tone. He hit the button to silence it then continued.

"Sometimes you have to make your own mistakes, Casey. And I don't think buying that property is one."

"You aren't hearing me, Murph. I agree, that is a great property. I'm just saying that you need to do more..."

Murph's phone again rang with Lindsay's tone. "Hold on, Casey, I'll tell her I'll call her back. Linds, I'm kind of in the mid... What? Are you both okay? We're on the way now, we'll be right there!" He hung up. "Come on, we have to go. Lindsay and Dawn were just shot at in the mall!"

3

GETTING "MALLED"

Lindsay and Dawn climbed into Dawn's Escalade and headed for some small independent shops both on and off US 13. They planned on hitting the new mall just south of the Maryland border and later going to a restaurant Dawn liked for a late lunch before returning to *Bayside*.

"I've been so excited about this, Dawn. I haven't had a 'girl's day out' since I moved to the Shore. Heck, I didn't have the money to do this until after we took second in that Virginia Beach tournament. I still can't believe we won first place at Rehoboth, and that you and I became friends there. I really wasn't looking forward to facing you then, or ever."

Dawn laughed. "You didn't do anything wrong; it was Murph that hooked up with you. I was so shifazzed when we met, I guess I was curious about who you were and why he kept pursuing you after he and I broke up. Nothing personal, but if I hadn't been so drunk, I don't think I'd have been up for meeting you. I can't believe I lived through the hangover from that night; it was pure agony. You guys earned that purse, you really out-fished everyone else. The publicity from it must have really helped your business."

"It has. We're booked for the last few mid-Atlantic tournaments, and we're fishing two Florida Keys billfish tournaments back to back in January. We have two in Palm Beach in February one in Stuart, and we're back home in March."

Dawn glanced over at her, smiling.

"What?"

"You just called ESVA home."

Lindsay laughed. "I didn't even realize I did that. But it is. I've never owned any real estate before, and it's good to be putting down some roots. I think the marina property will be a huge win for us." She noticed that Dawn didn't say anything. "What? You don't think it is?"

"I know a little about it, and yes it might be."

Lindsay's brow wrinkled. "Why do I sense a 'but' coming?"

"I'm not going to say any more about it."

"Why not?" Lindsay turned in her seat to focus more on Dawn.

"Because I don't think we should talk about it. I would have a hard time being objective."

"Because of Murph."

Dawn looked over at her. "Yes, because of Murph."

"Part of the reason I like hanging out with you, Dawn, is because you are a straight shooter. You proved that the night we met, and I feel like I can be the same with you. You are the closest friend that I have here, and we've only known each other for a short time. But up at Rehoboth when we got drunk that night you really opened up, and I appreciated that. It also made me see how much Murph hurt you. Even though I didn't know about you, after I found out what happened, my part in it made me feel like crap. But you also understood it for what it was, and since we both know Murph so well, that kind of gave us a bond, I guess. At least I thought it did. But if you don't feel right about talking with me, maybe we should head back and just call it a day. It's no fun being uncomfortable."

Dawn sighed. "You may not like all of what I have to say about Murph."

"I'm not going to apologize about him, Dawn. You understand a lot about Murph, and that gives you a unique perspective that I can't get from anyone else."

"True. But I might say something about him that makes you mad at me, and I don't want to lose you as a friend."

"I don't want a friend who can't be straight up with me. I'm asking for your advice because you know more about real estate than I do. I was a bartender last year and now I'm a fishing mate. I've made more money in the last three months than I ever expected to make in my entire life because of two tournaments. I've found the guy that could end up being long-term. I know I don't want to lose either the money or the guy. So, again, I think the marina property could be a huge win, what's your opinion?"

"You asked for it, so I'll tell you. We did an assessment of the property, and it could be very good, but it will take a huge investment. Much more than you've won this year. No bank will touch you two, with neither of you having any prior business management experience. Casey will go over all this with Murph this morning. We'll have to see how that goes; we both know Murph can be stubborn as hell. I'll tell you something that's probably the most important thing I could ever say to you; don't let your heart get in the way of your head when it comes to investing that money. You may never win another tournament, so you need to treat it like you'll never see another dime. Don't let Murph talk you into something that you aren't a hundred percent sure of."

"So, you aren't going to lease the restaurant. You don't think it's a great deal."

"As it sits now? No. But I'm going to let Casey and Murph talk things out and let's just see what they come up with." She glanced over at Lindsay and saw she was dejected. "Linds, let it go today, don't worry. Let the two of them talk things over. Casey won't let you make a bad investment or lose money. The important thing is you two have the property under contract and can control what happens to it. Now you can also decide the best way to make money with it. Because there is money to be made there, it's just a question of how to do it and how much you can make."

Lindsay first smiled dejectedly, then brightened a bit more. "At least I got you to open back up, I guess that's something."

"I guess."

THEY HIT a few of the smaller shops before they reached the mall a little before 11 am. Lindsay said, "I need a jolt of caffeine, and I'm buying."

"That's a deal. I want to shop a bit more before we head north for lunch."

The mall was a small one but had a decent group of fast-food restaurants in the food court. One was a good coffee shop where they each grabbed an expresso and sat at one of the benches scattered around the court. Two very pretty blond girls in their late teens sat down with coffees at a four-top table about ten feet from them, engrossed in their own conversation.

Lindsay said, "Not bad coffee, but not as good as what you had onboard up at Rehoboth."

Dawn nodded, "That's a special roast from Ocracoke Coffee. We pick up beans every time we go down there. It's the best little coffee shop anywhere, and it's always packed before 9 am. When you head south this Winter, don't forget that Ocracoke makes a great stopover on the way. Great harbor, restaurants, and coffee."

As they relaxed on the bench, they saw a girl who appeared to be a few years younger than the two other teens approach their table and sit down. From the looks on the older girls' faces, the newcomer hadn't been invited, and they apparently didn't know her. Dawn and Lindsay both could sense something was wrong with this picture and silently watched. The younger girl seemed nervous, and she was trying to strike up a conversation with the two. She kept reaching into her bag but would withdraw her hand when it drew their attention. Then a man and a woman in their thirties walked up and leaned against a column twenty feet away but directly within sight of the younger girl. The couple stared at the group. The man then appeared to be sending hand signals to the girl. When she wasn't having much luck befriending the other girls, the couple staged a loud argument, drawing the two older girls' attention away from the table. Dawn and Lindsay saw the newcomer reach into her bag and pull out what looked like a small squeeze bottle. She squirted something into each girl's cup while their attention was diverted. The couple quickly quieted down, and the girls turned back to their table, reaching for their cups.

Dawn yelled, "Don't drink that! She put something in your coffees!"

Lindsay pointed at the couple, "And those two are in on it!"

The younger girl now looked scared. "Lady, you don't want to get involved in this."

The older couple now was now approaching the table. The woman stared daggers at Dawn and Lindsay and said, "You two need to listen to her, and mind your own business." She spoke with an accent that Dawn couldn't place.

Dawn now jumped up to confront the woman as the two teenagers pushed their cups away from them on the table. Dawn said, "Lindsay, call 911."

The man reached the table and yanked the younger girl's arm, pulling the now terrified girl to her feet, knocking her chair over in the process. "Let's get out of here." He had a similar accent and an olive complexion. "And you stay where you are." He pointed at Dawn.

"That girl put something in their drinks, and she is obviously terrified of you. So, we're all staying put until the police arrive, and let them sort this out."

The man drew a semi-automatic pistol from inside his windbreaker and pointed it at Dawn, who grabbed her purse. She drew her own Sig Sauer nine-millimeter from a concealed holster on its side and pointed it at the man. Lindsay dove under a table, knocking it over and using the top for cover as the two older girls sat frozen in their seats. The crash from the table distracted and startled the man, who turned slightly while pulling the trigger. His shot went wide and missed Dawn by mere inches. With other shoppers in the background now fleeing behind the man, she couldn't safely take a shot at him. She knocked over another table and took cover behind it. The man and woman made a break for the exit, dragging the terrified younger girl with them. Now with their backs to Dawn and their attention on the exit, it allowed her to get up and go after them. She dove behind a concrete column just as the man turned and shot again. More screaming shoppers were fleeing as the second shot rang out. She watched helplessly, peering around the column's edge as they made their way out of the glass exit doors. Dawn couldn't move yet since there was no cover between her and the door. She figured she would be a sitting duck if she tried to follow them before they got farther away. Through the big plate-glass windows next to the entrance, she saw them all load into a gray minivan with dark tinted windows, the nearest vehicle in the parking lot. Then she dashed toward the door to get the tag number. Suddenly the glass in the outer door of the vestibule exploded as the man shot from the now moving van. Dawn hit the floor sliding on her stomach as another large pane next to the vestibule came raining down in tiny pieces after also being hit. By the time she picked herself up off the floor, the van had disappeared.

"Dawn! Are you all right?" Lindsay came running up.

"Yes, but they got away, and I didn't get the tag number. Let's go back and make sure those girls are okay."

They found out that one of the baristas had pulled the two girls over and behind the counter to shield them after the shooting started. They were unharmed but very shaken up. Somehow their two cups of coffee had remained upright on the table, preserving the contents. Two minutes later several sheriff's deputies swarmed the food court, with guns drawn. After discovering that the shooter and his crew had fled, they separated all the witnesses and started taking statements.

Sheriff Billy Albury, Kari Albury's cousin and Casey's soon-to-be ex-brother-in-law, quickly arrived on the scene. He always liked Dawn, but with the family entanglements of late, he now had a somewhat reserved opinion of her.

"Are you all right, Dawn?"

"Yes, Billy, I'm lucky the guy was a lousy shot. I took off after them, but I had to take cover and never got the license plate."

"So, what exactly happened?" After she related her story, he shook his head. "You're just damned lucky you didn't get shot. What the hell were you thinking, going after them like that?"

"That young girl was with them, and there's no way it was by choice. She was terrified, and they literally dragged her out with them, she wasn't going on her own. I had to try to get her away from them, Billy."

"Your carry-concealed weapons permit is for your own protection, not for you to play cop! You're just lucky that you didn't shoot back and hit a bystander."

She bristled at the dressing down. "Lucky, like hell! I held my fire on purpose because I saw there were innocent people in the background! If there hadn't been, you'd have had a body added into the mix."

Dawn's even temperament was disappearing with this exchange. She was approaching a level that Casey had once described as "redhead pissed," something that's rarely seen from her, and not a pretty sight when it is.

Billy was getting agitated too, "And you would be in handcuffs in the back of a cruiser until the State Police investigated and decided whether to charge you. That permit's not a license to play Rambo, and you'd be smart to remember that. Now stay put until my detectives are through with you. We've got a sketch artist coming down to put some drawings together." He turned and went over to where the two teen girls were sitting by the coffee shop and talked to them. A few minutes later the girls both came over to Dawn and Lindsay, who was still trying to calm Dawn down.

"Thank you both so much. If it hadn't been for you guys, we wouldn't have known about our coffee being messed with, and we would have finished drinking them," the one said.

Her pal added with a shudder, "Who knows what it was she put in them, and what would have happened to us. I saw there was something not right with that girl the way she sat down uninvited, but I never figured she might be dangerous. This is the Shore, nothing like this ever happens here."

Lindsay nodded. "These days you must accept that bad things can happen around here too, not just in the big cities. Always be aware of your surroundings and trust your gut instinct. Sad to say it, but you can't trust people you don't know until after they earn your trust these days.

"That couple had a funny accent, so they weren't from around here. Whatever those three were up to, it wasn't supposed to end well for you two."

The second girl said, "That girl wasn't from around here either, she had a New Jersey accent. She was really nervous, and now we know why. Those two creeps were watching her, and he had a gun on her the whole time. They must have forced her to spike our coffees. I wonder what she put in them."

Dawn said, "I'd be willing to bet it was some kind of date rape drug. Since they forced that girl to go with them, I bet that's what they had in mind for you two. They picked a day and time when the mall isn't that crowded, and they parked right by the door. There weren't too many people between here and their van, so they could get you to it easily. This has the feel of something that was practiced and planned." She was putting the pieces together.

"Dawn! Are you okay?" Casey came racing up with Murph and Kari in tow. He hugged Dawn tightly. The mall had been closed off, but Kari had talked her cousin into letting them in to be with their friends.

"I'm fine, Case. I'm just mad because I wasn't able to stop them." She related the story, including the part about Billy reading her the riot act.

"He was right you know. They could have killed you!"

"I knew what I was doing, Casey. That girl is someone's daughter, and she was terrified of those two. I wasn't going to let her get dragged away without at least trying to stop them."

Murph asked, "Are you two free to leave?"

"Not yet. We're supposed to work with that sketch artist after the two girls are finished with her." Lindsay was itching to get out of there.

An hour later they had given input to the sketch artist who used an app on a tablet to quickly and cleanly come up with three very accurate pictures. Billy finally cleared them to leave and said he would be in touch if he had any additional questions.

4

NEW PARTNERS

With shopping now the furthest thing from Dawn and Lindsay's minds, they all headed back to *Bayside* and *Lady Dawn* for a late lunch and hopefully an early cocktail hour. Once aboard, the yacht's chef made a seafood salad for the five, a welcome distraction from the events of the morning. After lunch, Kari excused herself to go back to the office, but Casey nixed that idea.

"Let's work over here on the boat. I'm glad you are here too, Lindsay, since you are Murph's equal partner, you should hear all of this too."

Murph, Lindsay, and Kari moved over to the couch while Casey and Dawn took individual chairs. Bimini had come over from the office and now lay at his old pal Murph's feet.

"Before all the craziness happened today Dawn told me you all wanted to pass on leasing the restaurant, but it still could be a good investment." Lindsay sounded curious.

Casey nodded. "That's right. Kari, you want to tell Lindsay what you told Murph this morning, so we are all on the same page?"

Kari sat next to Lindsay as she narrated the pictures on her laptop. It was obvious the concept intrigued Lindsay.

"I like what you've come up with but taking on a bunch of debt scares me." She glanced over at Murph, who nodded.

Casey leaned forward. "It comes down to this, you either put up your whole bankroll betting on a payout in a bunch of years with little or no income from it in the meantime, or you put up a fraction of that cash, give up some equity in what will be a much larger project and get part of a larger income stream. Meanwhile, your total equity grows to a much higher point than it is right now as the project pays back the loan and the property appreciates."

Lindsay still sounded doubtful. "Dawn told me that no bank would touch us because we don't have experience running anything like this."

"True. But we won't be going to a bank." Casey smiled.

"Who is 'we', Casey, and then where would 'we' go for financing?" Lindsay asked.

"That would be you and Murph, me, Dawn, and our friend and *Bayside* board member Eric Clarke. Plus, we would like to bring in one other partner on this, Kari Albury." Kari looked at Casey, very surprised. Casey continued, "I'll finance the project myself until it gets up and running, which is part of what I bring to the table. Then after it has a track record of making a profit, we can refinance it."

Murph scowled. "You pulled that finance card bit when you bought me out of *Bayside*, threatening to foreclose on the whole deal if I didn't take your offer."

"Yeah, after you teamed up with my soon-to-be ex-wife to take control of my project away from me and to keep me from being able to get her out of it. Which I was willing to forgive, but I won't be if you ever throw it in my face again. I had chalked it up to desperation since you hated her so much. Plus I figured you needed the capital to hold you over while you built your charter business."

"Well, this is *my* project, and I'll decide if I want any partners."

Lindsay frowned. "I thought it was *our* project, and we would decide together. I'd like to hear more about how much we would have to put up, and what our percentage would be."

"It *is* our project Linds, but right now we have one hundred percent. We can still get someone else to rent the restaurant, and then we can keep the whole thing for ourselves."

"But that would leave us with little or no income from it until we sell at some point down the road. I want to explore all the other options including building it out and keeping it." Lindsay sounded exasperated.

Kari was caught between the two that were sitting on either side of her on the couch. The look she gave Casey revealed just how uncomfortable she was right then.

Murph was digging in. "You get how tough they can be down there with outsiders. The county probably wouldn't even let us develop that property beyond what it is."

Casey jumped in, "Kari is a native, and has some connections. As a partner, she would have some pull. She has an inside line on things." He nodded to her.

"The head of the board of supervisors is my cousin, Carlton Albury. He owns one of the two largest boat hauling ways in the county. There are a lot of big wooden boats that need hauling on a ways rather than a strap hoist because a ways can support older wooden hulls better and with less stress. *Mallard Cove* has the other large one. The current owner hasn't been marketing his boatyard business because, without a railway shuttle system to move the hauled boats around, he can only have one out at a time, leaving it sitting on the ways. The county approved and issued permits for the shuttle project several years ago, but he never got around to installing it. Taking that ways out of the picture would ensure my cousin wouldn't have any competition. The rest of the board listens to him, so I'm sure he could sell the idea of how having that property cleaned up, creating jobs, and generating revenue, would be a huge plus for the county. It would set a better tone as visitors get off the CBBT rather than how the old, dilapidated docks and building look now."

Casey saw the comprehension on Lindsay's face, just as he saw Murph set his jaw and silently dig in on his opposition to the idea. "You know what? It has been one hell of a day for all of us. I'm declaring an early cocktail hour to celebrate that neither of you was hurt, and you both are back safe and sound." He got up and crossed over to the salon's bar, mixing stiff drinks. After a couple of sips of hers, Dawn then excused herself to go grab a quick shower and change. She wanted to relax and get cleaned up from her slide across the floor at the mall's entrance.

Casey could tell that Lindsay wanted to talk to Murph alone, so he caught Kari's eye and beckoned her with a lean of his head. They walked through the glass door and out on the aft deck together.

Once outside with the door closed, he said, "I wanted to give those two time to chat. I understand Murph, and he will take a little time to come around. But eventually, he will."

"Casey, I'm flattered about being considered for the deal, but we both know an investment like that is way beyond my pay grade."

He turned and looked at her. "What, are you taking lessons from Murph now? You haven't even heard the details yet, and already you are shooting down the idea. We are talking about three percent. You wouldn't put any money down, and your investment downstroke will come off the top of your profit percentage until that part is paid off. I told you when you came here we saw great potential in you, and that you would do well with us. This is part of that. Kari, if I don't teach you anything else, always listen to all the details first before you accept or reject any deal. I tried to teach Murph that, but right now his pride is getting in the way, which is why we're out here giving those two some privacy. He's fortunate to have Lindsay. Did you see how eager she was to get the details? Maybe she can get him to listen to reason."

Kari said, "I hope so. I think that plan would be a moneymaker for the property."

"I figured that as soon as you showed it to me. You've got a knack for real estate marketing and development. If we end up building this project, you'll be spending some time going back and forth, I want you overseeing the build-out. We still need you involved with *Bayside Club Estates*, but I can see you have an emotional investment in *Mallard Cove*."

"Thanks, Casey. I like that it's right at the tip of the peninsula and that it would make a statement about how ESVA is all about having fun on the water, not just commercial fishing, growing corn, cotton, soybeans, and raising chickens. We have so much more to offer visitors and building that complex would be a great step forward." She glanced in through the glass door. "It looks like she might be making headway."

"If there's one person I know completely, Kari, it's Murph. He'll come around, but Lindsay will have her hands full in the meantime until he does. We'll do our part to help her until then."

"How so?"

"By keeping his drink topped off. He's more amenable to new ideas when he's had a few. Or a lot." He grinned at her, and she returned it.

"Got it."

"Ordinarily, I wouldn't care so much about gaining a partial stake in a property, but this is personal. I want to see Murph and Lindsay succeed. It's the same reason I wanted to stretch out the payments on his buyback. He's his own worst enemy, but in this case, he has to come to that conclusion on his own. Or at least think that he did."

She nodded and said "heads up" as Lindsay came out onto the deck.

Lindsay was shaking her head as she came through the door. "Casey, I can't tell you if we're going to be up for your plan or not. Murph is being kind of stubborn."

Casey looked at Kari, and she nodded then walked back into the salon to check Murph's drink level. He smiled at Lindsay. "I'm not worried. Lindsay, I'd like to do this deal with you guys, but only if both of you are happy about it. I think he'll come around in due time so, don't worry. The hardest part is over, getting the property tied up and at the right price."

She looked at him gratefully. "I like what you proposed, and I need to get him to see that it makes the most sense for us."

"He will. Just give him the space he needs to come to that conclusion."

She nodded. "You guys were tight for a long time."

"We still are, even if it doesn't always seem that way. I try to look out for him. He did the same for me trying to warn me about my second wife, Sally. Though it didn't seem that way to me at the time, either. But I'm happy that he decided to stick around here in the warmer months. And I'm glad that you two are together.

"For fifteen years Murph was responsible for my boats and properties, but never really looked out for himself. He bounced from girl to girl, and party to party. Seems like that's changing now, and it's a good thing. It's past time for it to happen. This is also part of why I think he'll come around on this deal. For a long time, I preferred to do deals on my own. I only took in partners when I couldn't swing it alone. So, I understand where his head is right now, where both your heads are. But I've learned that sometimes it makes sense to have partners involved. Especially when you want to be free to focus on more than one project, and the partner brings something that's needed or missing to the table. That's why Cindy Crenshaw is a partner in our *Bayside* group; she's forgotten more about the hospitality industry than most others will ever know. If we put up a hotel on your property, she'll make sure that it's set up properly and run well."

Lindsay looked through the glass into the salon just as Dawn walked up to Murph and sat across from him. Kari came out onto the deck, leaving those two alone. "I felt they needed some space, and that Dawn needed to talk to him by herself."

Lindsay looked at her, "Hopefully she has more luck talking some sense into him than I did."

DAWN LOOKED ACROSS AT MURPH. It was the first time the two had held a conversation alone since he had broken their engagement. He held his drink in his lap with both hands, clearly nervous and not knowing what to anticipate. What Dawn was about to say though was probably the last thing he expected.

"You're on the verge of really becoming a success, you know that?"

Murph was taken aback. "Thanks?"

"I mean it. You are building a good high-end charter business, at least from what I've heard. You recognized a great real estate opportunity, and you jumped on it. I guess you learned a lot from Casey over all those years you spent working for him. And Lindsay is a prize, probably the best part of your success.

"Listen carefully to me. Don't screw it up, Murph. Any of it, especially the Lindsay part. I like her, she's a good person. Don't let your ego or your pride stand in the way of becoming a total success. You could lose the charter business and the marina and there would always be another opportunity to replace them down the road. Not so much with Lindsay.

"So, here's the deal. Do I really want to be involved in a deal with you? Truthfully, no. Does Casey? Yes. Not because of the deal, though it could be a good one, but because of you. He wants to see you succeed. You're his friend, and you always will be. I want to see Lindsay succeed and be happy because she's my friend, and I hope it stays that way. From what she's told me, she's happiest when she's fishing with you on *Irish Luck*. We both know that's a tough life when it's your only income. You end up traveling around like gypsies and you can only do that for so long before getting burned out. So, I'm just going to remind you of one of Casey's rules: Never put all your eggs into one basket unless you have to. You have a great opportunity here, don't blow it. Instead of having to worry about somebody showing up to work to sell your gas and rent out slips up here in Virginia when you are fishing down in Florida, with this deal you won't have to be concerned with any of that. We'll handle all those headaches. You'll both have a good income from it because of your forethought in buying it. So, before you say no, just think about it. If not for yourself, then for Lindsay."

Dawn got up, refreshed her drink then went out to the back deck leaving a silent Murph pondering what they all had said to him. Bimini had sat up and rested his muzzle on Murph's thigh with a soft "Chuff." Murph looked at him and asked, "So, you're on their side too, Bim?" Bimini raised his head and grinned. Murph went to the salon's bar and topped off his drink before joining the rest of the group outside as Bim followed. They all looked up from their spots around the big varnished teak table.

Murph addressed the group, "Let's just say I'm not as much opposed to the idea as I was at first. How much do you think we can make if we do it your way?"

Kari opened a zippered notebook and took out some papers, sliding them across the table to Murph. "That's just an estimate of annual income. We can't figure operating expenses and total debt service because we don't know what you're paying for the property, and what the total build-out will cost. We would need to figure all that out before we can do a true Pro-forma projection for each partner."

Murph rolled his eyes and looked at Casey. "So, how much does that mean?"

"Whatever it is will be a hell of a lot more than what you would make selling only slips, beer, and fuel, and you'll be left with a bunch of cash instead of having your whole bankroll tied up. Plus, we'll make sure everyone knows it's your project."

Murph sat down next to Lindsay who looked at him almost pleadingly, and he nodded. "I guess this makes sense. It may mean a smaller percentage, but we won't have to wait to sell it to get some cash from it." He turned back to Casey. "We're in."

Casey smiled. "Good! We'll all run down there tomorrow with Kari and look the property over. At some point, you'll need to meet Eric Clarke, too, since we'll all be partners. You guys stay here tonight, then we can celebrate the deal and the girls coming home safe. We've got an empty stateroom for you, and you've already had a few drinks, so it's not a good idea to drive back tonight. Now you can relax and enjoy yourself."

Lindsay beamed at Murph while Dawn gave Casey a sly smile. She wasn't crazy about the idea of having Murph stay "under their roof" overnight, but she wanted both him and Lindsay to stay safe. Just then someone called Casey's name from the dock. Casey stood up and saw Billy Albury standing next to the gangway.

"C'mon aboard, Billy!"

He made his way back to them along the narrow side deck. “Had a few updates that I thought y’all should know about. They’ve identified that girl from this morning as a fifteen-year-old who was abducted from northern New Jersey two months ago. The kidnappers match the description of the pair that was with her today. They had used another girl to lure her away from a group of friends on the boardwalk up there.

“In our case, those two girls’ coffee cups were spiked with a very potent sedative which would have also made them nauseous before rendering them almost incapacitated. They probably would have headed to the bathroom by the front entrance where it would have been easy for the kidnappers and their accomplice to steer them to that van. I called the FBI in because it’s a multi-state case, and they suspect they are part of a human trafficking ring. Their Anti Trafficking Coordination Team (ACTeam) is on the way down from Newark.”

Casey looked shocked. “Human trafficking? Like prostitution?”

Billy nodded. “Potentially, either domestically or internationally. Human trafficking is the third largest criminal activity in the world. Prostitution, slavery, you name it. Girls are kept here or shipped offshore. Some are put to work in brothels, and others are sold outright as sex slaves.”

Dawn shuddered. “I really wish I had gotten that tag number. Sorry, Billy.”

“It wouldn’t have mattered, Dawn. We found the van an hour ago in a field a couple of miles from the mall, torched. Someone stole it earlier this morning up in Maryland. They must have pre-planned swapping out into another vehicle to get away.”

“We’re a long way away from New Jersey.” Lindsay looked at Billy questioningly. “Do you think they are working their way down the coast?”

“We aren’t sure. Though they likely have a safe house where they can keep the girls until they break them. They get them to a point where they can work them on the street or ship them offshore. They are worth more being passive.”

Murph shook his head. "What sick bastards."

Billy nodded. "It gets sicker, Murph. These girls aren't even considered all that young as far as this kind of thing goes because they're already teenagers. Younger kids are worth even more than teens. You should see what's out there on the dark web, it would keep you awake at night."

Casey asked, "Do you think their safe house is nearby?"

"Possibly. It's likely somewhere close to the Shore. There are so many places around with a lot of distance between houses. Doubtful that it's in or near a town. They would want a place where they could come and go without many prying eyes. There are a ton of farmhouses around that are exactly like that.

"Anyway, I just wanted to bring you all up to date on where we are and tell you that if you run across any of the three again, don't confront them, call 911." Billy looked straight at Dawn, who nodded resignedly in return. "I've got to get back to the office and meet up with the ACTeam when they arrive, they'll probably be around here for a while."

5

BEER-THIRTY-BUNCH

Later that afternoon back at *Mallard Cove* the usual members of the daily Beer-Thirty-Bunch were starting to assemble. Bill Cooper, captain of the *Golden Dolphin*, came through the sagging screen door of the closed restaurant's porch and nodded to his friends who were already there. He was holding a six-pack of Busch beer in one hand and had a new unlit cigar in the corner of his mouth. "Hey, boys."

"What took you so long, Baloney?" Kim "Hard Rock" Collier loved needling Cooper about his nickname almost as much as Cooper loved giving it back to him.

"Well, Hard Rock, some of us musta had more fish ta clean than you. Bigger ones, too!" Hard Rock was Collier's latest nickname, the older ones having been forgotten after "the incident." Earlier in the summer Collier's original charter boat, the *Kembe*, had ended up on the rocks on one of the Chesapeake Bay Bridge-Tunnel's manmade islands after her steering had failed. Insurance replaced her with the *Kembe II*, complete with the old boat's signature orange paint job on her fifty-five-foot Carolina hull.

"In your dreams, Bill. We limited out early, much earlier than you! Pass me a beer."

"I guess next you'll want me ta feed ya, too. Hey, Gaffer, is he yankin' my crank or what?"

Fred "Mad Gaffer" Everett, Kim's mate, shook his head. "Got on 'em early, Bill, and loaded up fast. We were back two hours ago. 'Course this new boat is faster'n any around, 'specially the *Dolphin*."

"Yeah, well, my rig may not be that fast, but at least she misses the rocks and goes in the right direction! Speaking of that, why didn't ya tell me you were on 'em?"

Hard Rock smiled. "You didn't ask."

"Oh, now I gotta ask? See if I share info with you again."

Just then Jack "The Ripper" Greyson arrived, with his usual six-pack of Heineken beer in hand. A world-renowned maritime artist, his studio was a corner of the salon in his current boat, a sixty-foot custom sportfish called *Reba* where he lived aboard with his wife of several decades, Carol. The *Reba* was the latest in a long line of vessels that they had owned and lived aboard. A few years ago, one had even been an eighty-five-foot fireboat. They had arrived that summer with several hoses spraying high into the air. Some said that Jack had an artistic flair, but others said he was just plain crazy. You never knew what kind of boat he and Carol would show up in for the season; they traded them like cards in a poker game.

But in any case, Jack and Carol were fun. They were in their early sixties but could easily pass for being much younger, both in looks and in actions. The cockpit of the *Reba* was lined with Astroturf and filled with cheap lawn chairs. In the corner was a huge Yeti cooler that was always filled with ice and Heinekens. You didn't need to ask for one because if you were welcome aboard their boat, you knew you were always welcome to grab a beer and a seat.

"Got your panties in a wad there again, Billy?"

"You should be one ta talk about something getting in a wad, ya tightwad! For six years I've been asking you for a painting for Christmas, but nooo."

"And every year but this last one I've given you framed pencil sketches that I've drawn just for you."

"Yeah, *unsigned* ones!"

"If I'd have signed them, Bill, you'd have just sold them."

"Well, of course, I would've! That's the point! Unsigned they're worthless!"

"Nope, my art is just as valuable to me unsigned as if I had signed them. Each is a personal piece I created just for you and Betty. And don't forget, I *did* sign last year's present."

"Yeah, a plastic double-walled ice bucket with a paintin' of the *Dolphin* on the inside. How the hell can I ever sell that, Ripper?"

Jack sighed. "You just don't get it. Do you know how hard it was to paint that on the inside in reverse? All the fine detail had to go on first, then get covered with the base color. It was the hardest thing I've ever painted."

"And worthless! Though it does hold ice pretty good."

"Don't forget there, Baloney, I *did* give you the tuna tower from one of the old *Reba's* a few years back. And speaking of being a tightwad, when are you going to add controls up there?"

"You just wanted ta get it off your boat. An' I had ta bend the hell out of the front legs to even get it to fit the *Dolphin*. And I'm never going ta add controls up there. Scares the hell out of me being up that high just at the dock."

"Then why did you want it?"

"Because on them slow days when we don't limit out or we get skunked, I send my charter's kiddos up there on the ride back in and it saves the tips every time! Plus, I needed it as a place ta put Santa every year."

Jack shook his head. "And people call *me* crazy."

"Never ta yer face, Jack!" Baloney grinned.

Through the screen, they all had a great view down the marina's western basin. They saw Timmy O'Shea, known to the group as Spud, pass through the basin's breakwater in his twenty-six-foot bait skiff, the *Rum Runner*. He tied up in front of the building and quickly joined the group, empty-handed. He was slightly balding and of medium height with a paunch and was in his early thirties, yet he could pass for being much older. His Fu Manchu-style mustache always seemed to need both a trim and some fertilizer.

"Hey, who has an extra beer?"

Bill handed over one of his. "When are you goin' ta clean that scow, Spud? It reeks!"

"I just washed her down!"

Hard Rock jumped in. "Use a brush and some soap next time."

Spud looked disgusted. "My boat works for a living, and it doesn't have to smell nice like those 'wuss wagons' you guys run. No tourist is ever going to ride in it."

Hard Rock snorted. "No wonder. Any tourist that gets downwind of her is not going to want to get any closer."

"Hey! Without me, you guys would all be stuck using artificial lures. I've got the best baits around and you know it. I make you guys look like heroes."

Bill said, "Yeah, marlin come from miles away just ta jump on your baits. No skill on our part at all ta find them."

"Glad you finally admit it, Baloney!"

Robert Childers, whom they had nicknamed "Wall Street" walked through the door, followed closely by Bill's mate Bobby. Everyone in the group had gotten tagged with nicknames, and Bobby's was "B2" meaning "Baloney 2." Unlike so many of the others, B2 tended to be quiet, probably because he was used to not getting a word in edgewise with Bill on the boat. It was hard not to like Bobby.

Wall Street was another case altogether. While he was quiet too, it always seemed like it was just so that he could listen in and pick up information, even though he didn't fish. He lived aboard a 1977 forty-two-foot Bertram flybridge motor yacht on the commercial side across from the *Robert E. Grisham*. His nickname as well as his boat's name, *Bull Market*, came from his vocation as a day trader, which is why he claimed he wanted the privacy of tying up in the other basin. But there was something about the guy that just screamed "smarmy." None of the others could recall how he ended up as a part-time member of the beer bunch a couple of months ago. But at least he usually brought his own beer, like today. He looked over at Baloney, "Hey, Bill, did you find out anything about the place selling?"

"Yeah. It's a done deal, Wall Street. Murph and Lindsay got it all tied up."

Hard Rock looked concerned. "What are they gonna do with it?"

"Said they are gonna keep it pretty much the way it is, other than rebuildin' the docks and puttin' in new fuel pumps and tanks. Sounds like we can all keep our slips."

Hard Rock said, "Good. So, we don't need to start looking for another place to tie up. And I hope they get a faster fuel pump; this one takes forever. Nothing worse than sitting around for half an hour while you take on a hundred gallons." Hard Rock and Baloney were the biggest diesel customers in the group.

Bill nodded. "They ought ta know that firsthand, but I'll remind 'em. I know he used ta have something ta do with *Bayside* up in Accomack county, but I don't know if either of 'em has any experience with runnin' a marina. The more we can point 'em in the right direction, the better off we'll all be. And if they fix the restaurant, that's gonna bring in more business off the highway."

Spud grumbled, "Yeah and that'll take away our patio."

Hard Rock looked thoughtful. "Think they might be up for building a captains' lounge? A lot of marinas have 'em now you know."

Bill replied, "I'll ask Murph, but I don't know how deep their pockets are, and how much they're willin' ta sink inta this place. That'd be nice ta have though, 'specially in the winter when it's too cold to be out here. Might be a good thing ta help attract new slip renters." He looked out through the old screen enclosure at the basin and its crumbling docks and wondered how much would really end up changing. True, he'd like to have more charters, but what and how much they would all have to give up in order to get them was the question. Time would tell.

6

MOVING FORWARD

"Do you two always party as hard as this every time?" Lindsay moaned as she woke up next to Murph in a guest stateroom on *Lady Dawn*.

Murph rolled over and faced her, looking like hell. "Ugh. Only when we win tournaments, or our women get shot at." Despite it being midweek, the four had continued drinking until after midnight, and this morning they were paying the price for it.

"I'm willing to bet that the chef already has some high carbohydrate breakfast waiting upstairs." Sunlight was creeping into the portholes.

They emerged from the stairway ten minutes later, and Murph was correct, chef Shauna had anticipated their condition and cooked accordingly. Casey and Dawn were already sitting at the crew's table in the galley, working on a huge stack of pancakes and a pitcher of freshly squeezed orange juice. Dawn looked up at Lindsay, "How'd you sleep?"

"Like I was dead, then I wanted to die after I woke up. How about you?"

Dawn chuckled. "About the same. I needed to blow off some

steam, and also needed the coma that came afterward. Yesterday morning is not something I'd like to repeat anytime soon." She patted the booth cushion next to her for Lindsay, ensuring that Murph would have to sit over by Casey, as far away from her as possible, which he did. Bimini got up and walked over to Lindsay as she sat down. He lay on her feet and sighed.

Murph looked at Lindsay, "Looks like you have a new friend. You should be honored." Then he looked at Casey, "So, what's the plan for today?"

"Kari is already down in Cape Charles, having a breakfast meeting with her cousin Carlton. She wanted to run the concept by him for his approval before there was any chance of word of the project getting out. Then, assuming that goes well, we'll meet her over at *Mallard Cove* to all walk the property together. Sometimes opportunities and barriers stick out better in person than in pictures." Casey looked from Murph over to Lindsay. "Are you both still good with this idea?"

Lindsay nodded, and Murph said, "Yeah. You were both right, about a lot of things. Sometimes it's better to let the best people for the job do their thing, it's just tough admitting when I'm not one of them."

Casey shook his head. "That's where you're wrong, Murph. You were the best person for the job of figuring out this is a valuable property that's being underutilized. You saw the potential to unlock hidden value, but you were just trying to do it with limited resources. When you went looking for a restaurant partner, you were already taking the next step toward fulfilling that value. Together, we can build something that helps create an income stream for you two, so you can concentrate on what you love to do, tournament fishing. Murph, in all your years on the docks with the private boats, what's the biggest gripe that you've heard among the crews?"

Murph grinned as he realized where Casey was headed. "They don't get to fish enough because their boss is always too busy with work to fish."

"And you, my friends, are about to start investing instead of working your butts off, leaving you plenty of time to fish. I'm certain that you'll end up making much more off any sale down the road because of the improvements that get made. But in the meantime, you'll also be getting income without the headaches, so you might not be in a hurry to sell. So, show me the downside."

Murph grinned. "Just like the old days, Case, except now you'll be maintaining our project instead of the other way around."

Casey nodded. "Exactly. We'll just wait to hear from Kari, then we'll head on down. Once we look it over we can put together a partnership agreement and get started."

KARI CALLED AN HOUR LATER, telling Casey that Carlton was on board with the plan, and assured her that he could get it approved. Just as she predicted, he loved the idea of having the only large ways on ESVA and was drooling over the idea. The project approval would definitely get fast-tracked.

Casey rode with Murph in his truck, following Lindsay, Bimini, and Dawn in her Escalade. Pulling in from the highway, Casey looked over the entrance which was overgrown. They parked next to Kari behind the *Irish Luck*, and Casey noted that the *Kembe II* was still in her slip, with no charter booked today. The *Golden Dolphin*'s slip was empty; her signage including an old weathered fiberglass Mahi mount served as her placeholder. The Mahi had several layers of spray can enamel where Bill Cooper had done his annual "touch-ups." The result was something that looked less like a real Mahi, and more like an abstract modern sculpture.

"So, this where the *Golden Dolphin* ties up." The sign amused Casey.

Lindsay asked, "You know Bill, Casey?"

"I know of him, Lindsay. Quite a character, from what I've overheard on the radio when I was out fishing. Sounds like he would be a good draw for the docks. Kind of like the friendly 'Quint' character of the Eastern Shore."

A loud laugh came from the cockpit of the *Kembe II* where Hard Rock was busy replacing line on several reels along with Mad Gaffer. Open dates during the charter season didn't always mean downtime. Hard Rock grinned up at the group in the parking lot. "Sorry, didn't mean to listen in. But don't let Baloney know about that Quint comment, he'll want us all to start calling him that."

Murph laughed and extended his arm toward the cockpit of the *Kembe II*. "Casey, Dawn, Kari, this is Kim Collier and Fred Everett, otherwise known as Captain Hard Rock and the Mad Gaffer." They both waved from the cockpit before they went back to cranking on new line. "So, where do you guys want to start first?"

Casey said, "Let's identify the property corners so we can get an idea of how much land we have to work with. Kari, did you bring the measuring wheel, surveyors' tape, and the metal detector?" After she nodded he said, "Hopefully we can find the metal corner pins and mark them."

As the group in the parking lot started off toward the highway, Hard Rock looked at Gaffer and commented, "Wonder what's up with that? I thought it was only supposed to be Murph and Lindsay in this deal. That Casey guy sounds like he's running the show today."

"Sure sounds that way, Hard Rock. Maybe after they leave, we can find out somethin' from Murph 'bout what's really goin' on."

Two hours later Murph and crew came back to the *Irish Luck* for sodas and in Bim's case, a bowl of ice water. They sat around the cockpit on the covering boards discussing what they found while Bim leaned against his new pal Lindsay who was busy scratching him under his chin.

"I can't believe how far back the property goes into those woods. This is so much larger than I originally thought. Kari, I can see now why you said you thought we were underutilizing it." Lindsay was one happy buyer.

"Casey taught me as well that you have to let the property 'talk' to you, and then you'll be able to see what it's best suited for. I love this piece, and I'm so happy that you guys believe my plan for it is a good one."

"Yeah, no more reservations from me. I'm excited now about the whole thing. So, what's next, Case?" Murph was now eager to get started asap.

"I think tomorrow you, Lindsay, and I should fly over to Northern Virginia and let you guys meet Eric Clarke, our other partner. Dawn and Kari can work at *Bayside* drawing up the partnership agreement and registering the corporation while we're over there. I'll get the title company started, and hopefully, we can get this closed next week. Then we'll get a crew in here cleaning up the scrub at the front and taking out the trees over on the north side that need to go.

"I'll get our marine contractor down here right away and get him drawing up plans for the new floating docks. One thing that sticks out to me is there's no reason to have two separate basins since we aren't going to have a boatyard and commercial side anymore. So, that way we can dig out the divider and pick up even more slips. And since we want to promote all the charter boats, we'll put in some fish cleaning tables with roofs and lights over here just past the *Golden Dolphin*'s slip. It'll be the first thing anybody sees as they are walking down the dock. There's no better way to get a potential charter to open their wallet than having them see a bunch of fish getting cleaned right next to charter boat row. We'll add a few benches behind it, so people can sit and watch."

Murph nodded. "Bill will love that since it'll be right next to his boat. That'll be a better advertisement than his Mahi sign."

Dawn looked around. "Okay, we've accomplished everything that we wanted to get done this morning so, let's go find some lunch. Kari and I have a lot to get done between now and tomorrow when you guys get back in the afternoon. Casey, are you going to fly the Aerostar, or have the crew fly you guys in the Citation?"

"Aerostar. I want to see if we can spot any bait schools in the bay on the way back. Might want to fish Saturday morning. Plus, it's been a while since Murph and I flew together. Seems like old times. Kind of like when we bought *Bayside*, but this time without that crazy pot smuggler trying to kill us."

"Yeah, no troubles ahead on this one, Case. This should be smooth as silk." Murph raised his soda can in a toast as they all stood and joined him then headed for their cars.

GAFFER HAD BEEN on the flying bridge of the *Kembe II* repairing some faulty engine gauge lights and had overheard the whole conversation over on the *Irish Luck*. He pulled out his cell phone and dialed. "Hey, you know those favors I owe you? I think I can clear the books. You won't believe what I just found out..."

THE BEER-THIRTY-BUNCH WAS GATHERING as usual, and Baloney was one of the last regulars to arrive. He could see that Hard Rock had something on his mind. "What's up?"

"A lot. Murph wasn't straight with us about what he planned to do with the place. He was showing a bunch of people around today, and they were marking property lines and stuff. Gaffer overheard them saying they are going to take out the divider and make it one big basin. They're gonna nix the commercial side and put in more docks. And it sounds like they are gonna build something that's gonna take a bunch of land. They're gonna clear some of the woods in a week or two. Plus, they said something about a charter boat row. And get this, Eric Clarke is in with them. As in, *billionaire* Eric Clarke."

Baloney sat down and looked thoughtful. "Well, show me where the bad part is. If they're gonna have a charter boat row, I'd bet we're gonna be front and center on it. Murph said I can keep my old slip after th' construction's done, and I trust him."

Gaffer spoke up. "He said he was gonna put in a new covered fish cleanin' table with some benches behind it for tourists, and that you'd love it 'cause it's gonna be right next to the *Dolphin*."

"See? I told ya I trust him."

Ripper said, "Well, you can ask him again because here he and Lindsay come."

Murph and Lindsay opened the sagging screen door and felt like they were walking into a cooler. All conversation had stopped, everyone's eyes were on them and there was a chill in the air. Murph looked at Baloney and said, "What?"

"I hear ya didn't tell us the straight story about what ya have in mind for *Mallard Cove*."

"Whoa! I did, we did." He looked at Lindsay, who had moved in close on his side. "But a lot of things have changed in the last two days. I can tell you what those changes are, but you're going to need to keep it to yourselves for a bit."

Bill's unlit cigar moved from one side of his mouth to the other. "Okay, what's gonna happen?"

Lindsay spoke up. "We've brought in a few partners. Friends of ours who are real estate experts. Instead of a long-range plan of slowly fixing up the marina, it's all going to get done as soon as possible."

Lindsay looked at Murph who then asked, "If we wanted to build up the marina business and help everyone's charter bookings, what do you think we would need?"

Hard Rock answered. "A place for charters to stay, eat and drink."

"Exactly what our new partners thought, and what we plan to do. Not just one but two restaurants and bars. A decent-sized hotel, in-and-out storage for smaller boats, new faster fuel pumps, and concrete floating docks. Plenty of parking, a new fish cleaning station, beach volleyball by the beach bar, and a huge pool that overlooks the marina. A place where people want to spend a weekend, or even a week. Our target customers are going to be your target customers. And we're going to put on a couple of fishing tournaments each year, too."

Wall Street wasn't happy. "What about the commercial side? I like my privacy. And what about the *Grisham*?"

Lindsay answered. "The *Grisham* isn't the sort of business we're looking for, and she has to go before the floating docks get installed. We're getting out of commercial dockage as well as the boatyard business. We'll be taking out the ways and the divider and making it one big basin with only one inlet. But I'm sure whoever owns the *Grisham* won't have a problem finding dock space over in Norfolk. And don't worry, we're going to have a section of the docks that will be gated just for people that don't want to be bothered by tourist traffic. They've got that up at *Bayside*, and it works great for them. Some of the same people who own and operate *Bayside* are our new partners, and they'll be managing this place for us. But Murph and I will still be based out of here probably two-thirds of the year, and we'll own a big chunk of it."

Wall Street still didn't look happy. Ripper, however, looked thoughtful. He nodded. "This could all work. It'd be nice to have a couple of places to eat and drink here where we didn't have to drive."

Murph said, "See why we're bringing in partners? This place will be fantastic, and there'll be plenty of business for everybody! Our partner Casey Shaw is flying us over to NOVA in his plane first thing tomorrow morning to meet with another one in his group. So, things are gonna start happening pretty fast after that. We should close on the property next week, then we'll clean it up and get this old restaurant fixed up and ready to open as soon as possible."

Baloney looked worried. "About that. Since we're gonna be losing our afternoon meeting place, any chance you could add a captains' lounge in this grand plan?"

"Good idea, Bill. I think we can add that in don't you, Murph?" Lindsay smiled and the tension level on the porch all but evaporated with almost everyone. She looked over at Murph, who nodded. This whole concept and plan would work great, especially after getting everyone behind them. They didn't want to lose any of the current slip renters other than the *Grisham*, especially not Baloney or Hard Rock, their only two regular charter boats. Technically *Irish Luck* was now only open for multiple-day charters through referrals, and for tournaments. They wanted to help the *Golden Dolphin* and *Kembe II*'s business grow, so they could add other charter boats to the marina without poaching their business. Charter boat row would be a focal point of their marina operation. The hotel, restaurants, and bars should help draw plenty of new customers for them.

Eventually, the conversation drifted from the plans for *Mallard Cove* to Bill's charter today. While they didn't limit out, they brought back in some nice cobia and released a huge shark. Murph finally got around to mentioning yesterday's excitement, and Lindsay related the whole story again.

"I saw that on the news last night, but they didn't say who it was. You're just lucky ya weren't killed! Thank God you're okay. Ya say that girl was kidnapped from Jersey?" How Baloney pronounced Jersey sounded closer to Joisey.

"Yeah, and the poor girl was terrified. Who knows what those two have been doing to her."

Hard Rock asked, "And the redhead that you two were with today chased after them with a pistol? She's going to be a partner here? Sounds like one tough woman."

Murph replied, "You don't know the half of it, Hard Rock."

Lindsay laughed. "But Murph does! They used to be engaged. And she broke his nose once. Now she's my pal."

There was a lot of chuckling on the porch and Baloney asked, "So, what happened, Murph?"

"It's a long story, but basically, Lindsay happened." Murph blushed.

"I thought you said you and the redhead were pals. But you were the reason they broke up?" Ripper was confused.

Lindsay nodded. "I was part of it, but there were other things, too. I knew nothing about her at the time. It was later that she and her current fiancé Casey helped expose a tournament cheater, so we ended up winning the Rehoboth tournament. She and I got rip-roaring drunk that night on their boat in the middle of a huge storm. We figured out we had a lot in common other than Murph. We've been friends ever since that night a few months ago."

Ripper was shaking his head. "Now all of you are pals."

"Oh, I didn't say that! She still hates Murph."

"But you all are going to be partners?"

Lindsay nodded. "Funny how things happen, isn't it?"

Ripper chuckled. "Like that song says, 'truth is stranger than fiction it seems.'"

7

TOUGH TAKEOFF

The next morning Murph and Lindsay met Casey at the Accomack County Airport a little before nine. His Piper Aerostar 601P was waiting on the ramp in front of the office. Casey was talking to a man who bore a striking resemblance to a younger Sam Elliot, the actor.

"Lindsay, this is Sam Knight, the head of Shaw Air, our charter service. And Sam, you've already met Murph."

"Good to see you again, Murph, and nice to meet you, Lindsay. Y'all have a great flight this morning."

Casey said, "You guys ready? I've already done the pre-flight inspection and we're all set. Lindsay, you climb onboard first."

Lindsay climbed up and over the folded pilot's seatback into the single seat in the second row. Normally the Aerostar would have two seats in that row in addition to the third-row bench seat, but Casey had one removed for easier access to the back. It also left more room for Bimini's custom-made dog bed which was empty today since he was back at the office with Dawn. Murph boarded after Lindsay, taking the co-pilot's front right seat. Casey followed, sliding his left pilot seat back before strapping in. He then closed both the lower and upper parts of the "clamshell" style door.

Casey started both engines and taxied out next to the runway while going through his pre-flight checklist. After doing engine run-ups, he checked for incoming traffic and pulled out onto the runway. He firewalled the throttles and watched as the airspeed increased. The Aerostar was one of the fastest prop planes built and cruised at two-hundred-seventy-five miles per hour. Because of its high-performance, thin wings, it had a high takeoff speed of one-hundred-fifty miles per hour.

They were just passing through the hundred-mile-per-hour mark when there was an explosion on the right side. The wing dropped, and flames were shooting out from underneath as the wingtip came into contact with the ground. Casey shouted, "Hold on!" as he fought to keep control of the aircraft. The drag from the wing and the right propeller blades hitting the runway caused it to do a ground loop and it spun to the right violently, skidding sideways and off the asphalt. It threw all three of them forward and sideways against their seatbelts with that sudden deceleration and change of direction.

By that point, Casey had already chopped both throttles and applied full left rudder and left brake, but to no avail. The added side torque now collapsed both the nose and left main landing gear as the plane slid sideways on its undercarriage. The left engine mount broke, allowing the Lycoming power plant and what was left of the triple-bladed propeller to break free and end up being dragged between the fuselage and the inboard leading edge of the wing.

After what seemed like an eternity but was only a few seconds, the plane came to a stop in the weeds and a cloud of dust and smoke off to the right side of the runway. The right wing was engulfed in flames, and the left wing was now leaking high octane avgas. Both wings were basically big fuel tanks, and there was a third tank underneath their feet in the main fuselage. Casey figured they had just seconds to get out before the whole thing became a fiery inferno. He opened the top of the door, but the bottom part wouldn't budge.

"The door bottom is jammed, we'll have to climb over it. We've got to get out NOW!" He half climbed over, half fell out of the fuselage, then reached for Murph's hand as Lindsay screamed.

"My seat belt buckle is stuck, I can't get out!"

Murph reached in his pocket for the Buck knife that he always carried. Fortunately, since they were on a private aircraft, there had been no TSA security screeners to confiscate it. He climbed over his seat, halfway into the back, noting that the intense heat of the fire was already melting the plastic window next to Lindsay. His razor-sharp blade easily sliced through the webbed belt, and he then grabbed Lindsay's arms, pulling her over the pilot's seatback which was still upright. Casey reached in and dragged her through the half-opened door and around the loose engine. Then she helped him grab Murph's arms, and together they pulled him through the opening.

Casey yelled, "Run! We've got to get clear of the fuselage, that center tank is only half full, and it's going to blow!" They had gotten about seventy yards away when the tank ignited, the extra oxygen in it creating a very violent explosion. It created an orange and black fireball that rose rapidly upward, mushrooming as it climbed toward the sky. They kept running as the rest of the airplane became engulfed. Casey spotted Sam Knight's pickup speeding toward them ahead on the runway. Sam pulled up and was out of the cab before the truck was even stopped.

"Are you all okay?"

Casey nodded. "We're just shaken up. I don't understand what the hell just happened."

"I was watching you take off, and just opposite the ramp, something exploded in the right main's wheel well, I saw the flash. It took out the whole strut and wheel." Sam pointed back down the runway where that landing gear could be seen, lying on the asphalt. "Whatever caused that was unlike anything I'd ever seen before. I've seen gear collapse, but this one made a 'boom' as it did, and that tank ruptured simultaneously."

"Maybe the strut punctured it?"

"Nope, the strut went down, and the tank ruptured upwards. But the National Transportation Safety Board will get that all figured out. I'm just glad y'all are all right. Climb in, and let's get you back to the terminal." In the distance, they could hear sirens approaching.

. . .

"Casey, do you know of anyone who would want to kill you?" Sheriff Billy Albury had a very serious and concerned look on his face. An hour after the crash he was standing in front of Casey, Murph, Lindsay, Sam, and Dawn, who had rushed over after Casey called to tell her they were all okay. They were sitting in chairs in the private terminal.

"Kill me? Why? What have you found out?"

"We'll have to wait on the lab report to confirm it, but it looks like that gear strut was separated at the hinge pin by an explosive charge. I'm positive that somebody put a bomb on your plane."

Casey looked shocked. "We both knew some folks that wanted to kill me Billy, but they're all dead now. Your sister-in-law isn't happy with me, but she wouldn't do this. So, no, I haven't pissed anyone off this badly."

Billy shook his head. "No, Sally wouldn't have done this. It would have to be someone who had something to gain from one or all of you dying in the crash, and they'd have to be familiar with explosives. How about you Murph, or you, Lindsay? Do any of you have any enemies?"

They both shook their heads. Murph answered, "No, like Casey said, the only ones that might have been that upset at either of us was that crew of cheaters from the Rehoboth fishing tournament, and they died in that collision. So, nobody else that I can think of."

Billy looked thoughtful. "Did you see anything strange in your pre-flight check, Casey? Maybe something up in the wheel well?"

"No, nothing. Then again, I didn't climb up under it. The hinge pin is way up inside and is something that only gets checked during an annual inspection, and I just had it done last month. On the pre-flight, I'm just looking for strut and tire inflation, tread wear, brake pads, rotor thickness, and any leaking brake fluid. I didn't see any problems with all of that, so I moved along."

Billy said, "We also found some small pieces of what might have been a cell phone detonator. This makes sense because to make the biggest impact the bomb would have had to go off when you hadn't yet reached takeoff speed but are already going fast enough to destroy the plane."

"I was at about one hundred miles an hour when it happened, fifty miles per hour under my takeoff speed. Thankfully we weren't going any faster than that, this was violent enough. Wait, so you think that whoever did this was watching us and remotely detonated the bomb?"

Billy nodded. "We checked the security camera recordings, and about four am someone dressed in a hoodie and a Halloween mask walked up and shot each lens with silly string. You know, that stuff kids play with. They hit the ones that face the hanger and the North edge of the ramp which also covers the woods next to the runway. We searched those woods and found a spot where someone had been sitting for a while. There was a small pile of cigarette butts there, a brand that is made and sold only in Turkey. So, it's likely whoever did this is Turkish, or spent some time in the region. Is this ringing any bells with you three?"

They all shook their heads, but Dawn looked up with a startled face. "Billy, that guy the other day at the mall, remember I said he had a funny accent? It *could* have been Turkish. I haven't been around too many people from there, so it didn't click. But now that I think about it, that's probably it."

Lindsay furrowed her brow as she thought about it. "That makes sense. It sounded like a cross between Greek and Middle Eastern."

Billy took out his smartphone and pulled up a video of a man with a Turkish accent.

"That's it, that was the accent we heard!" Dawn exclaimed, and Lindsay nodded in agreement.

"So, it's possible you weren't the target, Casey. Maybe Lindsay was. But why? There were a lot of witnesses that day, and this is a lot of exposure and effort to put into silencing just one. It doesn't make any sense. And how would he have known who you were? We never released any names. How would he have known that you would be on this flight today? Who else knew who would be aboard?"

Casey thought it over. "Just the folks in our office and our boat crew. But they're all trustworthy and have been with us for a while. They wouldn't have had any reason to mention it to anyone else."

Murph looked over at Lindsay who shrugged and said, "The only folks we mentioned it to were some of the other boat crews at *Mallard Cove*. But none of them are Turkish, and they couldn't have cared less."

Billy nodded. "Well, if you think of any others, or if someone acts funny around you, call me right away. This was supposed to have killed one or all of you, so they may try again. Keep your eyes open and be aware of your surroundings at all times. I'll contact those two girls that were targeted at the mall and give them the same advice."

"I'm going to go one better, I'll get Rikki Jenkins to put someone with each of you Lindsay and Dawn until this gets sorted out and Billy catches this guy." Casey was as serious as he ever was. Murph look at him and nodded.

"You really think that's necessary, Casey?"

"Yeah, Lindsay, I do. We were only about ten seconds away from it not being necessary. For any of us. It's just a good thing we're all fast runners."

An hour later Casey, Dawn, Lindsay, and Murph walked into the McAlister & Shaw offices to find Rikki Jenkins already waiting for them with two very rugged-looking men in their early thirties. Rikki hugged all four.

"Rik, I was going to call you." She was one of Casey's best friends, along with Dawn, Eric, and Murph.

"Billy already did Case. He said that you wanted some of my team to keep an eye on Dawn and Lindsay until this thing gets sorted out. You kids just can't stay out of trouble, can you?" She had a slight smile showing.

Dawn smiled and said, "It's not like we go looking for trouble, Rik.

But it's just usually right there waiting on us when we get up in the morning."

"Yes, I know. At least you have a sense of humor about it. You two..." She looked at Lindsay and Dawn, "... get shot at, and then you almost get barbecued, Lindsay. Remind me not to fish with either of you guys for a while. Murph, I know you are licensed to carry a concealed weapon. How about you, Lindsay?"

"Yes, he insisted I get my carry permit after we moved in together. We aren't carrying today because we thought we might go into DC, and they'll put you under the jail for having a weapon over there."

"Okay, when you get back to your boat, I want you both to put your weapons on, and only take them off to shower. That also goes for you two as well." She pointed at Casey and Dawn. "We still don't yet know who the target was, or why."

They heard a low-flying helicopter. Casey said, "That's probably Eric."

"I called to tell him what happened and say you wouldn't be making that appointment today. He said he'd clear his schedule and head over. He's staying for the weekend," Cindy said as she walked into the room. "I'm so glad you guys weren't hurt! Rikki said that Billy thinks it happened on purpose. Who would want to do that to any of you?"

"Beats me, none of us have any idea. This is Lindsay, and this is Cindy Crenshaw," Casey said.

"Nice to finally meet you, Lindsay. And to be able to meet you."

Lindsay smiled. "Ditto. Nice to be able to be met, too. It was close."

Two minutes later Eric Clarke came rushing through the back door and hurried up the hallway. He shook Casey's hand and pulled him into a man hug. "I saw the wreckage from the air on the way in. I can't believe you survived, much less that you are all still walking around." He turned to Dawn. "And I understand you were playing Annie Oakley! I saw the news about the shooting at the mall, but I had no idea that was you until Cindy told me." He hugged Dawn. "I almost lost two good friends and partners on two separate occasions, back-to-back. That's a new one on me."

"I never even fired my gun; I was too busy dodging the other guy's bullets. And they think Casey's accident might be related. Someone put a bomb onboard that took out the landing gear and one fuel tank."

The color drained from Eric's face. "Someone was trying to kill you too, Casey?"

"Not sure. We think he was probably after Lindsay, but that has yet to be confirmed. Eric Clarke, meet Lindsay Davis and Michael 'Murph' Murphy, your almost late new partners."

"Nice to meet you both. Really nice to meet you. Wow, some morning you guys had."

Murph answered, "It was interesting, that's for sure. I'm glad to be able to tell the story. It was a close one."

"Looked like they don't come much closer, Murph. You guys were all lucky," Eric replied.

"Tell me about it. I've had over a hundred hours riding in that plane with Casey, and he's never so much as scratched her. This was Lindsay's first ride in a private plane, and she never even got to leave the ground."

"Well, you all have something on me. I spend a lot of my week flying, and I've never been in a crash yet."

Murph recoiled. "Don't say that! You never want to tempt the fates with flying or with boats. We got off lucky today."

"But today's accident wasn't an accident, and like Casey, my flight crews are proficient and cautious. Though you're right, Murph, that isn't something to kid about. Sorry." Eric gave him a chagrinned look.

"No worries. I'm not planning on flying anywhere else anytime soon, anyway." Murph's phone rang, and he looked at the screen. "Excuse me, I need to take this. Hello? Whoa, hold on." He walked out the front door and talked haltingly and animatedly. Three minutes later he walked back in. "That was our seller, Vern Voorhees. Word got back to some guy named Glenn Cetta about our deal, and he just offered more than Lindsay and me. Voorhees also heard about what we plan to put down there, so now he's gone ballistic."

Casey looked concerned. "What did you tell him?"

"I said that we agreed to his last number, which wasn't that far off his first one, and reminded him that he approached us first. I said that we had a signed contract with the deposit now in his lawyer's escrow account, and if he tried to weasel out of the deal, we'd sue the hell out of him. I guess he originally thought he was taking Lindsay and me to the cleaners, and now he's figured out that he wasn't so smart. I said that he better be ready to close next Friday because we are."

Eric smiled. "If 'Birddog' Cetta wants that property, I'd say you made a very good deal."

Casey asked, "You know Cetta?"

"He's a commercial real estate investor, and I bumped up against him once, over my building in Fairfax. He was lowballing the seller, driving him nuts, and trying to convince him he was the only buyer for his building out there. This was back during the real estate downturn when none of the banks were loaning money on commercial real estate properties. Especially ones that needed a complete gutting as that one did. I knew the seller was desperate, so I jumped in at two pm and made an all cash, take it or leave it offer that expired at five pm. I also knew Cetta was circling around it, and I found out all I could about him, including that he's an avid deer hunter. It was the opening day of the season. I knew no serious deer hunter would miss the afternoon hunt of opening day, and he sure wouldn't have his cell phone on him. The seller started sweating when he couldn't reach Cetta to get a counteroffer, and we signed the contract at a quarter to five. Cetta went crazy when he found out about it, but like this deal, it was already sewn up tight. He called me every name you can think of.

"That man *really* hates me. I can't say as I blame him; my building is now worth well over three times what I have in it. You know the old saying; it's not personal, it's just business? Well, that's not true in this case. This *is* personal, and it will drive him nuts." He was grinning from ear to ear. "I heard that he's been buying up marinas in the mid-

Atlantic. His office is in Virginia Beach, so *Mallard Cove* is right in his backyard. To miss out on this one and find out I'm involved will just throw gas on the fire. I love it! Word got back to me that he was already upset that I was in with you on *Bayside*."

Casey looked amused. "Nice when you can get a good investment *and* tick the competition off at the same time."

Eric nodded. "Absolutely. But enough about business for now. How about I buy everyone lunch at *Rooftops* to celebrate you guys coming home safely?" They all agreed and headed across the driveway to the hotel with the two security guys in tow.

8

ANOTHER OFFER

"That was a great meal, as always." Eric was happy to see that everyone had relaxed after this morning's close call. He was also glad to have had time to talk with, and learn more about, Murph and Lindsay. He had heard a lot about Murph from Casey, but it intrigued him that Dawn and Lindsay had become friends. Most women would want the scalp of any other female that had come between them and their fiancé. But during their conversation, he discovered there was an unusual quality about Lindsay, something that he couldn't quite put his finger on. He suspected that it was what helped quell Dawn's initial anger and eventually convert it into friendship. Lindsay had a way of making everyone around her feel at ease as if they had known her forever, instead of only minutes or days. She was a beautiful young woman, but that external beauty seemed to be amplified by her friendliness. In her case, that old adage of "beauty being only skin deep" didn't apply.

"I can't wait until the restaurant is open at *Mallard Cove*. It'll be so convenient for Murph and me. Plus, if the food is half as good as this, it will be a great draw to pull people off the road and put more boats in the slips," Lindsay said.

"That's the plan, Lindsay. It's all about building traffic. It'll take a while, but we'll get there," Casey replied.

Murph jumped in, "Speaking of getting there, I hate to eat and run, but we have a charter for Saturday and Sunday. So, Lindsay and I need to get back and prep the boat. Eric, it was great to meet you, and I'm looking forward to seeing you again soon."

"Might be sooner than you think, Murph. I may hop down this afternoon to get a firsthand look at the property."

"Sounds great, we'd love to show you around. We'll see you then."

"WHAT DO YOU MEAN, they're alive?"

The heavily accented voice on the phone said, "Somehow they got out before the plane exploded. I didn't know because it had gone off the runway out of my sight. I saw flames over the trees and was sure they were all dead. It was on the radio that they didn't die."

"First you screw up at the mall, and now this. You better not mess up transferring the girls in this shipment, or else. I want them to look good and healthy when they reach the Middle East. Is the container ready?"

"We are bringing it to the farm today and will stock it with provisions. We will load the girls a few hours before it is delivered back to the boat." As much as he despised the American, he still feared him even more. He knew exactly what the "or else" comment meant.

"You need to be extra careful around the farmhouse. While it's a good distance from the mall, after you messed up there's bound to be more scrutiny on the Shore. The Feds have come down now from New Jersey. Make sure you two stay out of sight as much as possible. Thanks to you screwing up again, I've got to figure out a way to throw another wrench into this marina deal to keep it from happening."

The Turk stiffened at the rebuke but kept his tone as civil as he could. "Everything will go as planned."

The American replied, "Then that'll be the first time this week. So, you had better make sure it does."

The Turk nodded without thinking that it wouldn't be seen. The connection broke as the American hung up. He looked over at Elif who was sitting at the kitchen table in the farmhouse. She asked, "How angry was he?"

"Not as angry as me. He treats me like a dog, but I do all the work. One day I will no longer need him. Once I learn his contacts for selling the girls, then he will have a very unpleasant surprise coming." He kicked one of the table's chairs, sending it sliding across the floor. "I will now spend time with the girl, and I do not want to be disturbed."

"We should ship her in this group and replace her with another to use as the lure. They have her picture now; people will be looking for her."

"They have your picture now, too. Perhaps I should put you in the container and replace you! I will decide when she goes, and who replaces her." He stormed down the hallway into a room at the end and slammed the door.

Elif shook her head. This was not good, he was now putting his reckless sexual desires above caution for their business, and it could end up getting them all caught. She got up and headed for the door, wanting to take a walk in the fields until after he was finished. The girl screamed a lot when he was in with her, and not from ecstasy. Elif knew he should be breaking in the other girls and not spending so much time with just this one. But she didn't dare bring up anything about this favorite one again. She hurried outside to get out of earshot before the screaming began.

"Eric sure seemed nice. He doesn't act like he's one of the richest guys in Virginia. Then again, Casey and Dawn are pretty down to earth, too." Lindsay said.

They were almost back to *Mallard Cove*, and Murph was driving his truck. Lindsay's new bodyguard was following behind them in a black SUV.

"Yeah, I wasn't sure what to expect, but I should have figured Eric for being a good guy. Casey doesn't keep many friends, but the ones he does are all nice. He won't put up with idiots who are full of themselves, at least he never has in the sixteen years that I've known him. I've seen him tell more than one to take a hike. It's part of why he wanted to move here from Palm Beach; to get away from all the put-on attitudes."

Murph pulled into the marina and parked behind the *Irish Luck*. The SUV pulled in a couple of cars over on Lindsay's side. He looked out his window and saw the seller, Voorhees, making a beeline for him. "Uh, oh. Here comes trouble." He climbed out of the truck as the marina's owner closed in on him.

"You, sonofabitch! You conned me! I reread that contract, and I saw where you had your names plus 'and or assigns' as the buyers! You planned to flip this place all along, even though you knew I didn't want some corporation taking it over. Now I hear you want to take out the ways, too. That'll put my customers at the mercy of Albury, and he'll be able to charge them whatever he wants. You lied, Murph. I thought you and Lindsay were honest people, which is why I came to you."

By then Lindsay had joined Murph, followed by her bodyguard. She looked at Voorhees and said, "Murph didn't lie, and I didn't lie either. We will still own the biggest part of this place. We told you that we didn't want to run a restaurant, and you didn't either, or it would still be open. This place can't keep going like this; it's going to take a ton of cash to make it profitable again. And tying up all that land you had set aside for the boatyard that you never finished building is crazy. Keeping that ways operating for less than two dozen customers a year doesn't work. If Albury starts overcharging, then some other boatyard will build another big ways and give him a run for his money.

"We didn't have this all pre-planned, it just fell into place as we looked for somebody to lease the restaurant. And yes, we always planned to put it in a corporation. Our own. These days anybody would be crazy to have it in their own name because of the liability.

That's why we added 'or assigns.' We were always going to title it that way. Only now there'll be a few more folks in with us that bring experience in areas where we don't have it, and this will help us make it the success it can be."

"Nice try, young lady, but Glenn Cetta told me how this Eric Clarke works. He said Clarke's a shyster who was probably in with you from the start. He said you were playing me from the get-go. Glenn is willing to pay me more than you, and I'm going to take him up on that."

Murph was now getting hot. The emotions of the day's events were all channeling into anger. "Oh, yeah? How could Clarke have been in with us from the beginning when you approached *us*, not the other way around? We never even met the man until this morning. And did you explain to Cetta that we have a rock-solid contract already? Did he tell you the part about what can happen to you if you don't follow through on your part of that contract? And did he say he'd cover you in a lawsuit? So, who is playing who here, and who's the shyster? I told you that we are closing on this property next Friday come hell or high water, and I'm dead serious. Cetta can offer you all the money in the world, but you have to complete our deal, and at the price we all agreed to."

"So, what then? You turn around and cheat me by selling it to Cetta?"

"Nobody is cheating you, get that through your head! We're paying what we all agreed to, and it's not for sale after that! Especially to someone who's trying to get you to break your word by breaking our contract. You tell him he can go pound sand."

"Tell him yourself, he's on the way over here to get a better look around."

"He can look around all he wants, but he's wasting his time. We have 'equitable title' to this place, and we aren't about to give it up." Murph turned and stepped down onto the dock and then onto *Irish Luck*, followed by Lindsay and her bodyguard. All three went into the cabin's salon and sat down. Murph looked over at Lindsay who asked him, "What does 'equitable title' mean?"

"It's a real estate phrase meaning we have the right to close on this property. Don't worry, Voorhees has to close, he suddenly realized he left a bunch of money on the table so now he's ticked off. He'll get over it when he has that check in hand at the closing table in a week and he starts his retirement." Murph stood up and then went downstairs to their stateroom returning with their two Glock nine-millimeter pistols and holsters. He handed one to Lindsay then he hooked his on the inside of his belt in the back, pulling his shirt over it, as she did the same. The bodyguard nodded.

Murph chuckled. "I know you're supposed to blend into the background, but you haven't said a word. What's your name?"

The guy smiled. "I'm Tony. I'll be here most days, then Dave will relieve me tonight."

"Well, Tony, just a heads up, we'll be leaving the dock tomorrow at 5 am, picking up our charter over at a dock by Lynnhaven inlet then heading offshore. We should be back here by 7 pm. Same thing on Sunday. Gonna be a long couple of days."

"I've had longer. I love boats, so this will be an easy couple of days for me, Mr. Murphy. Plus, I would bet that if anything were to happen, it would be here at the dock, though I'll be ready out on the water too." His head snapped to the right as a man jumped onto the stern's covering board and then hopped down into the cockpit, landing with a loud thump. Tony was through the bulkhead door with his Glock pointing at the guy who put his hands up in front of him.

"Whoa! I only came to talk, Murphy."

"I'm not Murphy. And it's not healthy to jump onto someone's boat you don't know, uninvited."

Lindsay and Murph came out around Tony and Murph addressed the newcomer, a guy in his early fifties, about five-feet-six and balding. "Who are you, and what do you want?"

"I'm Glenn Cetta, and I have a proposal for you."

"Ah, 'Birddog' Cetta. Voorhees said you would be showing up, and this caps off a crappy day. He said you are trying to get him to break our contract, and that isn't gonna happen. You were trying to convince him that we were playing him, and now you want to make a deal with us? Why don't you get the hell off our boat and haul ass out of here."

Cetta smiled, showing a mouthful of blinding, over-whitened teeth, reminding Murph of a shark. He backed up against the transom, sitting down on the teak covering board with his phony grin intact. "You haven't even heard my proposal yet. A smart man listens to all his options before he makes up his mind. I'm willing to partner up with you, then you can ditch Shaw and Clarke."

"Well, Birddog, we've already chosen our partners, and there's no chance in hell we'd ever work with you. So, why don't you do what Murph said and get the hell off our boat. A smart man would have already done that." Lindsay had her hackles up.

"Oh, a woman with some spunk. I like that. We can make a great team." Cetta's grin morphed into a smarmy leer.

Lindsay looked past him over into the parking lot, focusing on a new Land Rover next to her car. "You don't listen too well, do you? Is that your ride?"

"Yes, you like it? Partner up with me, and maybe I'll throw one like it into the deal. You'd look good in one."

Lindsay turned and opened the tackle center that was built into the bulkhead. She pulled out two, four-ounce egg-shaped lead sinkers, handing one to Murph telling him, "I bet I can break that Rover's windshield with one of these."

Tony looked amused, and Murph grinned saying, "Five bucks says you can't!" Cetta looked on in disbelief as Lindsay wound up and let the sinker fly, clearing the windshield but making a loud thump as it landed on and then skidded across his roof.

"Hey, you crazy bitch, that's my car!"

"Yeah, and this is my boat, you dumbass, and you were told to get the hell off of it. As the man said, it's been a crappy day, and you didn't want to add to it."

"Babe, you were a tad high. You can use mine and try again." With a grin, Murph tossed her his weight as Cetta cursed then quickly got up and leaped to the dock.

Cetta let loose a blue torrent when Lindsay nailed him on his left buttock as scrambled to get to his car. He shouted, "You two haven't seen the last of me!" as he got in and slammed the door. Lindsay wound up again as Cetta jammed the Rover in reverse and she pretended to toss another weight with her empty hand. All three of them were laughing so hard they hadn't realized that Eric's helicopter was circling overhead until it approached to land over in the gravel near the ways. They climbed up on the dock and walked toward it.

"Hey, babe, was that a bad throw or did you miss his windshield on purpose?"

"It was on purpose. If I'd have busted it, he could have called the cops. And hitting him in the butt was on purpose, too. I guarantee that left a mark, and he won't be in a hurry to show it off. Bet it will hurt to sit for a couple of days though!" She had an ear-to-ear grin.

"For the record, Tony, I'm Murph, not Mister Murphy. And did you by any chance happen to see anything?"

Tony smiled, "See, what? There wasn't anything to see."

Murph nodded and chuckled again. "I saw a jackass beating feet out of here, but I don't know why. Other than I'm dating Babe Ruthless here, and she doesn't put up with much."

Lindsay wrapped her arm through his. "And don't you forget it!"

ERIC CLIMBED out of the helicopter followed by Dawn, Casey, and Kari. "Who was in that Rover that was setting a land speed record in reverse?"

Murph answered, "That was your buddy, Cetta. He had been sweet-talking Voorhees again, then he jumped on our boat, thinking he was going to talk us into partnering up with him. What an ass."

"Not my buddy, I guess he likes you better." Eric laughed.

Lindsay laughed. "Not anymore. Turns out he doesn't enjoy flying lead."

That shocked Dawn. "Tell me you didn't shoot at him!"

"Of course not! But a random seagull dropped fishing weights on both him and his car." Lindsay winked at her. "I don't think he'll be in too much of a hurry to trespass on our boat again."

Dawn shook her head as Eric chuckled. "That's great! Hopefully, he'll butt out now, and we can get this closed. I love how big this property is and the main road frontage it has. I can see why you snatched it up so fast. Kari pointed out the corners back in the woods from the air. Great job on the plan too, Kari, good use of the property. Now let's go look at the restaurant building."

They crossed over to the dock, walking past *Irish Luck* and the *Golden Dolphin.* Baloney was in the cockpit along with B2, having finished up a half-day inshore charter, and he looked up at the group. "Now this place is gonna go all upscale? Helicopters an' stuff? What's next?" He sounded disgusted.

"Relax, Baloney. It's only our partners looking things over." Murph introduced everyone from up on the dock.

"Hey, Bill, good to put a face with the voice. I own a Jarrett Bay called *Predator* and I've heard you on the radio a few times when we were fishing." Casey gave a small wave.

"Oh, yeah. Heard you out there, too. Nice rig ya got. Ya moving it down here?"

"No, we keep it up at the *Bluffs* or *Bayside*, depending on the season. We own both marinas. Have you been up to the *Bluffs*?"

"Nah. We've been pretty busy this summer. It'll slow a bit now though."

"Then take a ride up to the *Bluffs*, and you'll see what we'll be shooting for here. Though this project is much larger, and the hotel will take up a lot of the property. They're already installing the new floating docks up at the *Bluffs*, the same as what we'll have here. You guys have lunch or dinner up there on me and check out our food. Just give them this." He handed his card down to Bill.

"We'll do that, thanks." A relieved Baloney looked at Murph and nodded. "I see why ya brought them in with ya, Murph."

"I told you to relax, Baloney. You're gonna like what we'll do here, especially when it helps fill up your charter schedule."

"Yeah, just don't forget the captain's lounge."

Murph nodded. "Don't worry, we're going to talk about that up at the restaurant."

THEY SAT ON THE PATIO, admiring the view of the marina out through the screens. Eric asked, "What's this about a captain's lounge?"

"You're sitting in it. Most of the current slip renters get together here almost every afternoon, talking about fishing and drinking beer. It's one of the best parts of this place as it is now. It ties everybody together and helps form a sense of community among all the boat crews. They're concerned it's all going to stop when the restaurant reopens, and we need to make sure that it doesn't. I'd like to add an enclosed room next to this one that'll take its place and be something they can use in the winter as well. It'll go a long way toward keeping them happy when the bar is too packed to fit them all, and it'll be more of a draw for new charter boat crews, too," Murph said.

"Good idea. Bill's kind of an outspoken guy, isn't he?"

"You don't know the half of it, Eric. But he's a good guy and well respected by other charter boat crews all around here. When he talks this place up, there's going to be a lot of interest. That'll help fill our charter boat row quickly."

They took a quick tour of the restaurant building and then checked out where the outside bar and beach volleyball would be added toward the water. Then they walked to the other end of the building and Eric called over to Bill, "Hey, Baloney! Got a second?"

Baloney joined the group. "What's up, Bucks?"

Eric was taken aback. "Bucks?"

"Yeah, it's short for 'Big Bucks.' If you're gonna be around here, ya get a nickname, and that's yours." Baloney had a mischievous grin on his face. The nickname was also a test, to see how much of a sense of humor Eric had.

"Whatever. Okay, Murph came up with this as the site for the new captains' lounge. What do you think?" Eric had just passed Bill's test. And the view from the proposed addition would be right down the charter dock, allowing anyone inside to see all the fishing cockpits.

Bill looked it over and said, "Yeah, this'll work."

Eric looked at the partners, "Everyone else happy with this?" When they all nodded, he said, "Okay, let's get a picture of all of us with Baloney in the middle and the *Golden Dolphin* in the background. This will make a great publicity shot, and maybe we'll get some other captains thinking about how it's such a great location."

They got B2 to take the picture, so it would include all of them. In the center in between Eric and Murph and Lindsay was a beaming Baloney, who was going to get a lot of mileage out of it with other crews, which was exactly as Eric had planned.

9

MORE BANG FOR YOUR BUCK

Later that afternoon the Beer-Thirty-Bunch assembled as normal, though Murph and Lindsay said they would be a little late since they were still busy prepping for their weekend charter. That suited Baloney fine as he held court uninterrupted, bringing the rest of the group up to speed on the day's developments. Since Murph and Lindsay weren't there, he put a large emphasis on his part in things, including creating Eric's nickname.

"I'm telling ya, this is gonna be great for all of us! The week after the kids close on the property their new group is puttin' up a website about the place and the plans for it. As soon as the new docks are going in, they're gonna do a feature on social media 'bout the *Dolphin* and the *Kembe II,* promoting each ah us. Sounds like things're gonna start happenin' fast around here."

"Sounds like they already are. You sure got onboard fast. Bucks letting you borrow his helicopter or something?" Ripper loved needling his pal.

"Very funny. At least I recognize an opportunity when it hits me over the head. Not all of us are world-class artists that have a ton of magazines dyin' ta get an interview. Some of us work for a livin' and need publicity ta drive charter traffic to our boats. All that costs money, unless it falls into yer lap for free, like this did. An' don't forget they said they're making a gated dock for you snobby hermit types."

Spud walked in through the sagging door and took his normal seat. "What'd I miss?"

"Oh, not much. Baloney is now a billionaire's kiss-ass buddy and gets to borrow his helicopter on every other Tuesday. Wormed his way into a publicity picture with him." Ripper had a mischievous grin as he said it. "Even named the guy 'Bucks.' You know, like his own personal Daddy Warbucks."

Baloney frowned. "Bite me, Ripper!"

"What was a billionaire doing here?" Spud was confused.

Hard Rock said, "He's one of Murph and Lindsay's new partners. Showed up in a big helicopter. They're moving on this thing real fast. But the good part is we're gettin' a new captain's lounge next door. Sounds like a real sweet deal. To be honest, I don't see a downside to this thing, 'specially for me and Bill. Should help boost our business, and it's coming to us free, we don't even have to do anything."

Murph and Lindsay came through the door followed by Tony, whom they introduced as a friend. They brought a medium-sized Yeti cooler filled with ice and beer with them. Lindsay announced, "Beer's on us this afternoon, guys!" They had covered the bases with everyone's favorite brands, right down to Ripper's Heineken.

Baloney looked suspicious. "What's the catch?"

Spud looked at Baloney, disgusted. "What part of free beer don't you get?"

Murph laughed. "What? We can't buy our soon-to-be tenants and current friends a few beers without being suspected of there being a catch to it? We're just happy that things are going so well with all this, and that you guys are onboard with the changes. I'll admit, I wasn't that crazy about this whole hotel idea at first, but Casey made Lindsay and me see it made sense for us. For all of us, making this place more popular than it has ever been. So, this is about celebrating putting the deal in place with our new partners. Even though it really won't be complete until after Lindsay and I close on the property next

Friday morning for the partnership. But at least the hard part is over with. Oh, and we're celebrating living through the plane crash this morning."

Baloney's eyes bugged out. "That was you guys? I knew you said you were flying today, and I heard about the crash on the radio, but I didn't put two and two together. Are you guys all right?"

"We were shaken up, but we're fine now." Lindsay told the story as their friends listened intently.

"Geeze, girl, you get shot at one day, and almost die in a plane crash two days later. Time to buy a lottery ticket 'cause you've used up all your bad luck already!" Hard Rock shook his head, amazed.

Murph grinned. "So, it's free beer on crash day. Only because we're still around to buy the beer! And next Saturday night we're gonna have a cookout right where the new captain's lounge is going in, and everybody's invited. In fact, invite everybody you know from the other docks, and the Virginia Beach fleet too, we'll throw a huge bash."

"I get it, we're all gonna do a bit of promoting for you," Baloney said.

Murph shook his head. "Not just for Lindsay and me, but as I said, this is for all of us. You've heard the old saying: 'Build it and they will come? Well, I want to build it and have them already lined up to be here. The more people that find out about this place, the better off we'll all be. I want to build a 'buzz' about it and let everybody know what's coming."

There were nods throughout the group except for Wall Street, who didn't look happy, but who didn't say anything either. He sat back, listening and silently sipping his beer as always.

THE NEXT TWO days were indeed long ones, just as Murph had said. With the old Rybovich's cruising speed of twenty-two knots, it took over two-and-a-half hours just to reach the fishing grounds, even in only three-foot seas. But they were productive offshore as they got into the white marlin as their charter clients had hoped would happen. They released over three dozen in their two days of fishing. Then their clients asked to be kept up to date whenever "the bite" got that hot again and when they had vacancies in their charter schedule. It looked like their bad luck was indeed behind them as they pulled into the slip Sunday night, totally exhausted.

Murph woke up early on Monday, finding Tony in the salon after he had relieved Dave from the night shift. The fresh glazed doughnut he had in hand caught Murph's eye.

"That looks good. Where's it from?"

Tony nodded. "That little place on 13, about five minutes north of here. They were hot, just coming out of the fryer. Great coffee, too."

"I think I'll go pick some up for Linds and me. She's still asleep."

"Go ahead, I've got it here, Murph."

Murph climbed up onto the dock, seeing both crews on the *Kembe II* and *Golden Dolphin* getting ready for half-day inshore charters. He called over to them, "Hey, going for hot doughnuts and coffee. You guys want any?"

Hard Rock and Gaffer passed, but Baloney and B2 lit up at the thought.

"Got it. I'll be right back." Murph climbed into his truck before he remembered he had left his keys on the counter in *Irish Luck*. He hopped down into the cockpit then felt the pressure wave and heard the explosion from the bomb that detonated in his truck cab. It took out the truck's windows, scattering glass bits for over twenty-five yards. Tony came running out of the cabin, pistol at the ready as he looked up and down the docks.

"Murph, are you all right?"

"Yeah, Tony. I'm just glad I forgot my keys." Murph looked at the cab of his truck, which was now smoking from a small fire. "I better go put that out."

"Like hell! You better get into the cabin. We aren't sure that there's no one out there with a gun, too."

Lindsay came running out just as Baloney and Hard Rock were

yelling, wanting to find out if everyone was okay. She grabbed Murph. "Babe, are you hurt?"

"No, I'm good. I forgot my keys, or I'd have been in that." He looked over at his friends that headed over from the neighboring boats. "I'm good, guys."

Tony hustled both of them inside as he called 911, then grabbed a fire extinguisher and put out the cab fire. He also called Rikki and updated her. She told him to make sure nobody got near Lindsay's car, in case it was booby-trapped, too. He said he was already on it.

An hour later *Irish Luck* had been moved over to the bulkhead in front of the restaurant. They wanted to be away from Lindsay's car which was now the center of attention for the State Police's bomb squad. They had determined it did indeed have a similar device inside. The *Kembe II* and *Golden Dolphin* had both already left on their charters after their crews made sure Murph and Lindsay were okay. They had given statements to the authorities saying basically that they hadn't seen anything or anyone suspicious around the vehicles.

The salon of *Irish Luck* was now crowded with people, including Murph, Lindsay, Sheriff Roberts of Northampton County, a major from the Virginia State Police, Casey Shaw, Rikki Jenkins, and two investigators from the FBI ACTeam. Tony was up on the flying bridge where he had a bird's-eye view of anyone who might be approaching.

The lead FBI investigator addressed the group. "Okay, all the events of these last few days appear to be connected to the mall incident since it was the first one, but the question is 'how?' We are missing something because Mr. Murphy wasn't there until after the suspects left, and Ms. Davis had never seen them before. We never released her identity before the airplane crash, but someone had to have had it. Assuming these devices are connected, and we have no reason to think otherwise, it's looking like Ms. Davis might have been the intended target. You two are known to frequently ride together, so whoever did this might have set the one in the pickup in case you did today. Were you scheduled to go anywhere this morning, the two of you together?"

Lindsay shook her head. "No. But we probably would have gone out to lunch or dinner together; we try to get off the boat and out of the marina at least once a day. We usually take Murph's truck because it has more room. But I had no idea he was going anywhere this morning."

"I saw Tony's doughnut, so it was just a spur-of-the-moment idea to go get some for us, and some friends on the dock. Not something I do all the time."

The FBI agent scribbled on a pad as he listened. "Well, whoever did this probably already knows they missed. While we figure out why they want to kill you and until we find them, it would be a good idea for you both to keep your heads down. Do you have any other charters this week?"

Murph shook his head. "Nothing for the next two weeks, we blocked it out because of closing on the property in case the date got moved."

"In that case, I'd recommend you get away from here for a while and go somewhere where you might be hard to find. Meanwhile, we'll try to get this solved and apprehend those responsible for it."

THAT AFTERNOON through the patio's dilapidated screen Wall Street watched as an empty container trailer passed through the charter boats' parking area as it headed back to the road, having delivered its container. The *Grisham*'s deck crane had just unloaded the cargo container and placed it on her deck where it was secured in place in case of rough seas. He turned back to the rest of the group.

"So, does anybody know where they went?"

Baloney shook his head. "No idea. The *Irish Luck* was already gone when Hard Rock and I got back from our charters, an' my call ta Murph went straight ta voicemail. The cops took Lindsay's car and what was left of his pickup, so wherever they're headed, they got there by boat. I just don't get it though, why somebody would want to hurt those two kids?"

"What about that guy, Cetta? If either of them were gone, chances are the deal would be back up for grabs. That could be a motive." Ripper looked thoughtful as he said it.

Baloney replied, "He *was* pretty pissed after Lindsay nailed him in the ass with that sinker. But is that something somebody would kill over?"

Wall Street said, "I heard he wanted this place badly. The cops said that these bombs were put in their consoles and had timed delays that the interior light circuit activated. Whoever did this wanted them both to have time to get in, sit down, and get buckled up, so he or she is smart. Murph got lucky. If I were the two of them, I'd walk from this deal. It isn't worth dying over."

Ripper stared at Wall Street. "You seem pretty convinced this was all about the marina. What about the mall shooting?"

"I'm willing to bet that was just a coincidence. The cops didn't release their information, and by that point Cetta was already working on Voorhees, trying to get him to ditch the contract. Cetta is the only one that makes sense because he knew about them being in the deal. He was the one who had something to gain."

The Mad Gaffer was fidgeting, and beads of sweat were forming on his forehead. Hard Rock looked over at his mate. "Are you all right?"

Gaffer shook his head. "I used to work on Cetta's boat when I was first startin' out. He did me some favors over the years, and I was just trying to pay back those markers. I told him about Murph and Lindsay makin' the deal for *Mallard Cove*. And I told him about them goin' to fly with Shaw to meet Clarke. I didn't think he'd ever do nothin' like this; I swear! I didn't think it was him after the plane crash, but now..." His voice trailed off.

Baloney said, "You gotta tell the cops. He could still be going after them! At least now they'll know who it is."

"I still can't believe it. I mean, I seen him do some slimy stuff, but he never hurt nobody that I ever knew about."

Wall Street said, “It had to have been him. It all makes sense now that we are sure he had the info about them flying on that day. With Murph and Lindsay out of the way, he could snatch this place right up. I doubt he planted those bombs himself, so he might still have some kind of contract out on them, and they could still be in danger.”

Baloney fished the sheriff's card out of his wallet and dialed his office number. “Sheriff Roberts? Captain Bill Cooper here. Yeah right, Baloney. Listen, I just found out some things you need to know...”

10

A MISSED OPPORTUNITY

Late that afternoon *Irish Luck* pulled in past Shaw's *Lady Dawn* and tied up on the private dock side of *Bayside Resort*. Casey quickly hopped aboard, telling Murph, "Bill called and said to tell you quote, '*Turn on your damned phone.*' He has an update to give you."

"Baloney has an update? On what? And how did he know we were here?"

"Your beer bunch thinks they figured a few things out. I'll let Bill fill you in. He doesn't know for sure where you are, he just figured that since we're all partners, I'd be talking to you at some point."

They went into the boat's salon where Murph called Baloney and put him on speaker. "Me an' Wall Street solved it. Turns out Gaffer used ta work for Cetta, an' he told him all about yer deal and yer plane trip. The sheriff is hauling Cetta in now for questioning. Gaffer 'bout lost it after he found out he almost got you guys killed, he never thought Cetta would do anything violent. He's pretty busted up over it."

Murph harrumphed. "Not as much as we almost were. I'm gonna talk with him, face to face when we get back. Even if he thought Cetta was harmless, he had to have known at the very least it could cost us our deal."

Baloney's normally gruff voice was softer. "Murph, I've known Gaffer fer a buncha years. He didn't mean nothin' by it, he was just trying ta repay some favors ta his old boss. Gaffer would do the same for you. He just didn't use his head."

"And almost got us killed in the process."

"Hard Rock is worried now that you'll kick the *Kembe II* outa the marina over this, or if he keeps Gaffer workin' for him."

"Who he keeps on or not is his call, and no, we aren't kicking them out of the marina. But Gaffer better learn to keep his mouth shut."

Baloney sounded relieved. "I don't think you need ta worry about that anymore. He's made himself scarce ever since he told us what he did. And he did 'fess up on his own after we all started ta figure it out. You could see it hit him; he got really upset."

Murph nodded. "Good. We'll let him stew on that for a bit before I talk to him. Oh, hey, Sheriff Roberts is calling, I gotta go. Thanks, Bill." Murph answered the second line. "Hi, Sheriff, I hear you caught the guy."

"Word travels fast around here, but in this case, it may be premature. The state police are here questioning Cetta, but some things just aren't adding up right for me. He's admitted wanting to break up your deal, and that he has a signed backup contract in case you don't close. He also said that your wife hit him in the, uh, hit him with a sinker, is that true? The state boys think both things give him different motives for wanting to harm or scare you and her."

"That's not true. We're not married."

The sheriff grunted instead of laughed. "Okay, what about the rest of it?"

"I had no idea he had a backup contract."

"What about the assault? Did that happen?"

Murph smiled at Lindsay. "Sheriff, have you seen any evidence of this alleged assault?"

"I haven't asked him to drop his drawers if that's what you mean."

"Then I'd say he probably fell in the parking lot and landed on a rock. And we don't own the property yet so that would be between him and the current owner's insurance company. But if he's blaming Lindsay, then I guess that could be the motive."

Billy grunted. "Motive for embarrassment, but probably not enough to want to blow someone up. That's what I mean, this is way too violent an act. He'd have to know that he'd be a suspect. Plus, he owns several other properties including five other marinas around the mid-Atlantic. I doubt that he would put that all at risk over a little personal vendetta. Planting bombs isn't a spur-of-the-moment thing; it requires planning and a certain amount of skill, especially to avoid getting blown up in the process. Bombings are designed to draw attention to things rather than to be used as quiet leverage. They aren't good for business, especially a business you want to buy. I know I asked you before if you knew anyone who would want to harm or kill you, but we haven't gone at it from the idea of someone wanting to harm your business."

Murph shook his head, "What about the bomb on Casey's plane? That couldn't have anything to do with the business."

"Maybe not hurt your business, but it would keep your deal from closing, and open it back up to negotiation. So in that way it would." The sheriff sounded like he was thinking it through while talking it over.

"So, now you're saying this might not be related to Lindsay being at the mall."

"I'm saying that I'm trying to think about this from every angle that I can. There's still way too much that we don't know. But after listening to Cetta, I don't think he's our guy. So, this means you need to still keep your guard up. And you need to tell me if anything comes to mind, even something simple, small, or just out of place. Call me any hour of the day or night."

"Got it, Sheriff. We'll be in touch if either of us thinks of anything." Murph hung up.

Lindsay looked at Murph. "So, I guess we'll be here for a while."

"No, I think we'll move *Irish Luck* back when we close so that we can get ready for the party."

She was taken aback. "You aren't seriously still thinking about hosting that now, are you?"

"We have to. Bill has already spread the word around about it. I even heard about it on the VHF radio when we were offshore. If we cancel now, word will get out fast that *Mallard Cove* is a dangerous place to be. We can't afford that. It's bad enough about the truck bombing, but at least everyone has heard they've identified a suspect. So, I was going to meet with Kari while we were here to see if we couldn't get some 'Under Renovation, Opening Soon' signs for the restaurant and marina. I want to get them installed Friday after we close on the property. Maybe have an artist's rendering of what they'll look like on those signs, too."

Casey spoke up, "I have to agree with Murph on this one. We can't afford to look like there could be any more trouble."

Lindsay bristled. "Easy for you to say, being an hour away."

Casey shook his head. "We'll be right there with you. Dawn and I are bringing *Predator* down for the weekend and are going to stay aboard. We figured that the more sportfish boats we have there, the easier it'll be to sign up new ones. Plus, we would never leave you hanging like that, Lindsay. We're friends as well as partners."

Lindsay looked embarrassed. "Sorry, Casey, I've just been on edge..."

Casey interrupted her. "Don't apologize or give it another thought. After what you've been through, what we've all been through, everybody is on edge."

"Thanks."

Casey waved his hand in a "no worries" way, smiling at her and nodding. "Hey, about this shindig you two are throwing, you do realize it's a promotional event for the partnership, right?" Murph and Lindsay stared at Casey with blank looks. "We all benefit from it, so the new company should pay for it. And, one of the reasons I wanted you two to partner up with us is because we have the resources needed to make a lot of things happen. Like Kari and her sign guy, but also our event group."

Murph lit up, "Carlos?"

Casey nodded. "Carlos. Want to turn him loose on it? If you still want to do the cooking you can, and he'll just get it set up for you. Or you can turn it all over to him, tell him what you want, then you guys are free to mingle and work the crowd. That would reinforce you two as the faces of *Mallard Cove* and be a better use of your time."

Lindsay gave Murph a hopeful look, and he nodded then said, "That would be great, Case, so long as it's not too 'over the top.' Just a good barbeque setup that everyone will be comfortable with. No caviar and champagne."

"Murph, when have you ever known me to eat caviar or drink champagne? Sushi and top shelf rum and vodka is a different story though." Casey grinned. "Let's go talk to Carlos, and you two can tell him exactly what you want. He'll handle everything from the tents to the tables and chairs."

LATER, Lindsay and Murph ate an early dinner at *Bayside*'s *Beach Café* after they met with Carlos. They had a corner table by the beach, and it had a great view of the upcoming sunset. Each had a half glass of wine left from their dinner bottle. Murph was caught off guard when Dawn appeared, standing beside him.

"You guys mind if I sit for a minute?"

Lindsay smiled and shook her head as Murph looked beyond Dawn, expecting to see Casey.

"It's just me, Murph. Casey's back on the boat. I wanted to find you guys and invite you over for some wine and to watch the sunset if you are up for it."

Murph stayed silent as Lindsay said, "We'd love to, thanks, Dawn. Wouldn't we, Murph?"

He looked at Dawn. "Yeah, sure. But I'm kind of surprised he's not with you."

"That's because this was my idea, Murph. I was the one who wanted you guys to come over. Both of you." She saw the surprise on his face. "Here's the thing. As much as you hurt me, and I was madder than hell over it, there were even times I thought I wanted you dead after you broke things off. But then I faced that being a real possibility not once, but twice this week. I realized that like it or not, we're still friends, and I'd have hated it if you had gotten hurt or worse. I really would have. It surprised me, too.

"You know, Murph, things always seem to end up working out how they should for both of us. We can't always see that, especially when we're in pain over something, but it's the truth. You two are a great couple, and I'd have hated to lose either one of you. After I almost did, it cleared my vision a bit when it scared me. So, come on over to the boat and watch the sunset, like some old and new friends. Ones that have been through a lot together in a short time. Let's celebrate still being able to watch a sunset together."

Murph looked at Dawn's face and saw total sincerity. Not knowing exactly what to say he nodded, then downed his half glass of wine.

Dawn asked, "Fortifying your courage?"

He shook his head. "Nope. Just too cheap to leave it on the table." He grinned at her, and she returned it.

OVER ON THE top deck of *Lady Dawn*, Casey was waiting in a teak lounge chair with his own glass of wine. *Lady Dawn's* steward, Andrea O'Neil, was bartending, and she handed a full glass of wine to each of the trio as they arrived and settled into their chairs.

Casey looked over at Murph and nodded, knowing what Dawn had planned to tell him. He was glad that the bitterness between those two was subsiding, at least for the most part.

"Hey, when you had your phone off this afternoon, was that so you couldn't be tracked?" When Murph nodded Casey said, "It doesn't work that way anymore. It used to be that you just had to remove your phone's battery and it couldn't be found. Now, with the batteries glued in, that isn't an option anymore. And turning it off doesn't help, either. With your battery in place, a halfway decent hacker can still track you." He passed a couple of black nylon bags with Velcro strips over to a curious Murph. "Faraday bags. We keep some around the office and in our cars. Drop your phone, tablet, and any other electronics in there, roll the top closed and seal it with the Velcro, and you're completely off the grid. At least as far as anyone trying to track you or eavesdrop on you is concerned. It completely blocks all incoming and outgoing signals, and the phone doesn't know where it is, or where it has been. Rikki put me onto these; they're nice for when we go out looking at properties and don't want to do our competition's scouting for them." He grinned.

"Thanks, Case! Very cool. What do I owe you?"

"Nothing. They aren't expensive. As I said, we keep a few extras around the office, in the cars, and on the boats. Oh, and here." He passed him a couple of key cards with magnetic strips. "C3 keys, so you two can relax whenever you're here. After all, you helped design it."

C3 was the nickname for Casey and Dawn's private getaway place, set back in the woods behind a locked gate on the south side of the marina's parking lot. It had a huge enclosed "party cabana" with a pool table, steam room, bar, and sauna inside. Outdoors there was an infinity pool, spa, outdoor kitchen with a huge entertaining deck, and a stone fire pit, all overlooking the Chesapeake. They built it when Casey lived aboard his fifty-eight-foot Hatteras. While it might sound like a boat that size should have a lot of room, it was really designed for warmer climes and outdoor entertaining on the exposed decks. During the colder months, there wasn't a lot of room inside for larger groups. C3 was Casey's answer to this.

"Thanks again, Case. For pushing us to develop the property, too. Feels kind of like old times back in Florida."

"Except now you aren't working for me, and instead we're working together. It's going to be a lot of fun too, starting with the party Saturday night. We've got a lot of planning to get done in the next few days, not just for the event, but for the whole project. But let that wait until tomorrow, let's all just relax and enjoy the sunset. It's like having our own Mallory Square on the Chesapeake instead of over the Gulf of Mexico in Key West."

~

"THANKS TO YOUR BUNGLING, you missed them again. And now the cops have one of the devices, completely intact. And because you scared them off, now we have no idea where they are. So I have no way to prevent them from transferring the property."

"We could kill the old owner, patron, and that would stop it." Volkan's voice shook; he was clearly scared of the angry American.

"You don't think, do you? Killing the old man just means that his estate would still have to sell it to Murphy and Davis. The contract is still valid, and they'll push to close the deal to help liquidate the estate. It might cause a slight delay, but that's it. No, we need to do something to make sure that no one will want to have anything to do with that place.

"I have a plan. We need the name *Mallard Cove* to remind people of death and destruction so that nobody will want to go near there in the short term. It has to be a financial disaster. And this time I'll handle things since you can't seem to do anything right. There won't be any more screw-ups. When Voorhees tires of trying to sell it, I'll pick it up from him for a song when I'm his only option as a buyer. Meanwhile, we'll be able to keep operating from there, and I can build up more cash to buy it. Where are the materials for making the devices?"

"Here at the farm, in the workshop." Volkan hated it when the American came to the farm. The American did too, he wanted no one seeing him around there.

"I'll be up there in an hour, be sure to have them all together as well as the tools. I want to spend as little time there as possible."

. . .

An hour later the American pulled around behind the farmhouse and headed into the workshop carrying a square plastic food storage box with a sealed lid. Thirty seconds later Volkan joined him. The American looked over the workbench.

"Where are the cell phones?"

"I had them in the house to charge the batteries, patron. The girl will bring them over."

The American set to his task, assembling the devices. He heard a girl's voice with a New Jersey accent, and Volkan replying. He turned and recognized the young girl from her wanted picture, the one from the mall. She was staring at him. Volkan saw the patron's face flush in anger, so he yelled at the girl to return to the house as he snatched the phones from her and handed them to the American.

"What is she still doing here? I told you to send her in this load, but she's not only still here, now she's running around loose? And she's seen my face!"

"I'm sorry, patron. There were no spots left in the load. Elif is watching over her—"

The American backhanded him and a small trickle of blood formed at the corner of his mouth. "She was supposed to be replaced by one of those girls, and you know it! Now the container is already on the boat, and we can't take a chance of switching them out over there. But you counted on that, didn't you? Get her chained back up, now! Then after I leave, take care of her."

"Please, patron, I have her well trained. She will do anything I tell her and will not try to run away. She fears for the lives of her family back in New Jersey."

"I'll bet she does whatever you ask, and that's why she's still here despite what I told you to do. Even though it's you who should fear for your own family. You know how long my reach is, and what happens when people don't do as I tell them. You can't keep her as a 'pet.' Get rid of her, or you'll be missing more of your people. Now get down to the boat and help with the transfer tonight. At least get that part right!"

11

FAST FIXES

The next day Murph and Lindsay joined Kari, Casey, and Dawn at their offices for a development meeting. Kari started it off. "Our first hurdle is getting the place looking better by the start of the barbecue. The parking lot is so full of potholes that it looks like it was hit by mortars. I don't think Voorhees has added any gravel there in years. Once we finish the construction, we'll be paving over that gravel base in all the parking areas. But in the meantime, I'll have truckloads of gravel, along with graders, standing by on Friday. As soon as the ink is dry on the closing documents, we'll start smoothing it out and fixing it."

Dawn said, "That's an easy and quick way to make a property look dramatically better."

Kari nodded. "That's not all. I was able to get our marine contractor to agree to pull his barge and crane off the *Bluffs* job for a couple of days and get into *Mallard Cove* by Friday morning. He'll replace a lot of those rotten pilings and start making some of those slips wider and longer. We'll have a bunch of slips renovated and available next week, well before rockfish season. I also have our electrician lined up on Friday to install several new shore power pedestals with dock lights. That'll be another nice upgrade that will happen quickly."

"So, by the time the party starts everyone will see things are already moving ahead. That's great, especially the dock lighting. The place is pretty dark at night; there's only a couple of pole lights that work, and that's a huge liability and security issue." Lindsay was pleased.

"Exactly. This will light up the dock section that will be freshly patched up. Then we can reuse the fixtures on the new floating sections after they are installed later. And we'll also have some renderings set up on easels at the party. They'll show the remodeled restaurant with its new outdoor bar that faces the beach and the captain's lounge at its opposite end. Plus they'll show the new marina layout with all the floating docks that are going to replace the wooden piers." Kari had a genuine and infectious enthusiasm.

Murph added, "With this crew that I hope will show up, seeing a bunch of dock maintenance already started and the crane barge still sitting in the basin will be very convincing. *Mallard Cove* has had a reputation for being so rundown for a very long time. We only ended up there with *Irish Luck* because it was all we could afford back then. We were actually in the process of looking around for another marina to work out of when Voorhees approached us to buy it. Trust me, the word will get out that things are getting better fast. Then once they get a taste of the food and drinks that Carlos' crew puts out, we'll turn this place into Southern ESVA's new home of its largest sportfishing fleet, and a great destination." Murph was caught up in the prospect of a reinvigorated business. Things were getting real, and fast.

Murph knew there was no way that he and Lindsay alone could have even attempted to pull off a party of this size in such a short amount of time. And you could forget about any of the marina repairs. Casey and Dawn had plenty of pull with the best ESVA contractors because they kept adding to a backlog of new projects, and they paid their invoices on time. Those were two things that contractors loved in their customers. That, plus the fact that they only wanted the best quality workmanship. Word of that had gotten around quickly after a couple of subcontractors were fired after they were caught trying to cut corners at *Bayside*.

By the end of the day, their group had accomplished everything from creating a logo to drafting a complete site plan. They also created budgets and set schedules. With the help of their marine contractor, they also designed the new dock layout, maximizing the number of slips in the enlarged single basin. Carlos joined in with the restaurant redevelopment plans, and a sketch of an additional restaurant and bar to be built simultaneously along with the hotel and the new boat barn. The property would finally be put to its highest and best use.

A LITTLE AFTER FIVE O'CLOCK, Lindsay, and Murph moved over to C3 on the pool deck by themselves with a couple of beers. Having all of the security that was in place at *Bayside* meant there wasn't any need for a bodyguard unless they left the complex. While they appreciated what the two men did, not having Tony or Dave nearby as a constant reminder of the danger they might be in meant they could relax a bit. Lindsay leaned back in her chair and sighed. "I hadn't realized how much there would be to this. I didn't know how complicated it would get."

Murph looked over at her, "We can still go back to owning it ourselves as only a marina, or we could flip it to them altogether if you want."

"What? No! That wasn't where I was going with this. I meant that I learned so much today. They've got a talented team, and we're lucky to have them all working with us. They came up with so many things I'd have never thought of. It's exciting, Murph, almost as exciting as catching a dozen white marlin. And I like doing both things."

"You two are talking about doing things you'd never thought of that are exciting? This sounds like a conversation maybe you should have alone." Dawn had walked up behind them and was grinning.

"What? Oh, I guess you came in on the tail end of that," Lindsay said with a chuckle.

"If you think it's exciting now, wait until you see the old building renovated with new ones added and then the checks start coming in," Dawn said as she pulled up a chair.

"That's the part I'm looking forward to, the checks." Murph grinned.

Dawn had a sly look. "You always were into instant gratification. Well, almost instant." She and Lindsay laughed.

"Hey! Not true, and you both know it!"

"Wow, someone sure is touchy about timing!" Lindsay needled him.

"He always was, Lindsay."

"So, this is how it's going to be when you two get together, and Casey isn't here to rein you in, Dawn?"

Casey said from behind Murph, "Oh, I'm here all right, Murph, but I'm smart enough to know not to try to rein her in. Something you never learned." He was grinning now, too.

"Har, har, har. I guess it's pick on Murph day."

Lindsay said, "We're thinking of extending that to a month, babe!"

Murph made a fake grimace face then nodded as he looked around at the three. He hadn't been sure about how this would work out, being partners with Casey and especially Dawn again, but he had a good feeling about it now, especially after his recent talk with her. That they could joke together was something that he never thought would happen again. It was funny the way some things work out. This time it meant almost dying for it to happen.

Casey said, "Speaking of extending something, you know I told Bill Cooper that I wanted him to try the food at the *Bluffs*. What do you all think about extending an invitation to him, B2, and their guests for dinner over there tomorrow night? I know he's already wound up over what we are doing, but it would be great to have him even more primed before the barbeque on Saturday."

Lindsay laughed. "First that publicity picture, and now he gets to be a dinner guest? He'll be talking about this for years, so yes, I think it's a great plan. Plus, it'll be fun. His wife Betty is a doll, and I don't think they get out much, so it'll be a real treat for them." Murph nodded in agreement with her.

Casey pulled out his phone. "I'll call him and set it up."

MARLIN DENTON PULLED his custom twenty-six-foot Gold Line outboard named the *Marlinspike* into his slip at Lynn's Marina in Virginia Beach. He carried both of the cobia that he and his charter client had kept over to the cleaning table, then filleted them and packaged the meat in plastic baggies. After collecting his charter fee along with a nice one-hundred-fifty-dollar tip, he headed back to the boat to wash it down and stow the tackle. Halfway back to the boat he was intercepted by the dockmaster, who handed him an envelope. Inside was a new dockage rate sheet showing a huge increase, effective the following month.

It shocked Marlin. "What the hell? A twenty-something percent rate hike?"

The dockmaster looked sheepish. "I know. It just came down from Mr. Cetta's office. He's raising prices at all of his marinas. But he kept the ten percent discount for an annual contract, only now you have to prepay the whole year upfront to lock it in instead of paying each quarter."

"What about my ten percent discount for having multiple boats?"

The dockmaster shook his head. "That was negotiated between you and the old owners. Mr. Cetta said he won't honor any other discounts from now on. Sorry, Marlin."

The marina had been purchased by Cetta earlier in the year, and this was the first time Marlin's annual dockage contract had come up for renewal since the sale. He had only budgeted for quarterly payments, which had been the norm in the past.

"I've got three boats in here, and this means my dockage will be going up by a third! That's like paying for an extra boat."

"I know. I'm sorry, man, but it's out of my control. Everything is corporate these days." The dockmaster turned and walked away.

Marlin looked at the figures on the paper again, then crumpled it up in a ball and threw it in the nearest trash can. There was no way he was going to take that much of an increase. It wasn't right, and he couldn't afford it. There were just a few months left before the winter season when his only income would be from selling articles to magazines. Business would pick back up in the spring, but until then dockage was his biggest expense, and having it increase by that much would be catastrophic. And he didn't have the more than ten grand in cash it would take to prepay an annual contract. Then he remembered hearing Bill Cooper say something on the radio about new stuff happening over at *Mallard Cove*, and about it being under new ownership. He figured it was worth a call. He took out his phone and found Bill's contact number.

"Bill? Marlin Denton."

"Ah, Shaker! What's up?" Marlin's Baloney given nickname was "Shake-n-Bake" which he sometimes shortened.

"Listen, I heard you on the VHF talking about new owners that are going to fix things up at *Mallard Cove*. They still have cheap dockage over there?"

"Cheapest around, at least for now. And these kids have a great plan for building a charter fleet out of here."

"But there's nothing around there."

Baloney smiled, even though Shaker couldn't see it. "There's a lot to this plan, and I'm happy to be in on the ground floor. You thinking of making a move?"

"I'm considering it."

"Well, if you're willing to move this way fast, I can probably help you lock in a great deal. You're talkin' all three boats, right?"

"Yeah. Everything."

"In that case, what are you doing on Saturday?"

"Not much, no charter booked yet."

"The new owners are throwing a barbeque shindig here that

afternoon. I can introduce you and lean on 'em fer you. We're pretty tight. One of 'em is Eric Clarke."

Shaker knew Baloney dropped Clarke's name to impress him, not realizing that it wouldn't work. Shaker was from the lower-income side of a family that had some high-income members. Higher even than Clarke. But that was something he didn't want to get around. People would figure that he was loaded too, instead of having to scrape during some months just to come up with his dockage.

"That's nice, Baloney, I'm glad for you. But I need lower dockage fees more than I need higher income friends."

"You just meet me at the *Dolphin* on Saturday morning, and I'll introduce ya. I can guarantee you are gonna like what you'll see. Oh, hey, one of those new owners is calling me right now. I'll see you on Saturday." He hung up and switched to the incoming call.

"What's up, Big Tuna?"

"Big Tuna?" This caught Casey off guard. He had the phone on speaker, so Murph and Lindsay looked at each other and laughed. It was classic Baloney. Bill heard them in the background.

"Yeah. I heard you were the one who caught the giant bluefin that won the Virginia Beach tournament this year. Nice going. Oh, hey there, Murph and Lindsay."

Both chimed in, "Hey, Baloney."

Casey replied, "Well, I was running the boat."

"Yeah an' running the boat's the same thing as catching it. Can't catch 'em if ya can't find 'em. So, what's up?"

"Would you, B2, and your ladies like to be our guests for dinner at the *Bluffs* tomorrow night, say around six? We'd like to show you all around, so you get an idea of where we're headed with *Mallard Cove*."

"We'll be there. An' I might just earn that dinner. I'm working on gettin' Marlin Denton and his three boats over here. You guys are gonna be around on Saturday morning, right?"

"We're planning on it."

"Good. I wanna introduce ya before the crowd shows up for the party."

Murph's eyebrows had raised. "Baloney, is this the same Marlin Denton that's the writer?"

"Yeah, as well as bein' one of the best guides in the lower bay. Got a flats boat for skinny water, and a center console outboard with a half tower for beach runnin' and rough water. Lives on a bee-you-tee-ful ol' Chris Craft." Bill's New Jersey roots were showing more than normal.

Murph nodded to the others, they definitely wanted him at *Mallard Cove*, he would fit in well. "Yeah, I read an article by him in the latest Mid-Atlantic Fisherman. He would be a great addition to the fleet, then we would have a choice there between big sportfishing rigs and outboards. That would appeal to a lot of people."

"That's what I was thinkin'. He's great with fly fishermen, too. He can smell a redfish from a mile away. Plus, he'd fit in with the gang. You're gonna like him, I guarantee it." With his Northern accent, Baloney sounded like that guy who sells men's suits on television.

Casey said, "That sounds great, Bill. So we'll see you tomorrow night at six. You know where it is?"

"Been ta the marina once, a few years ago."

"Remember, Bill, not a word to anyone about where Murph and Lindsay are, and where they are going to be tomorrow, okay?"

"Who, Tuna?"

Casey shook his head resignedly at the nickname. "Right. See you tomorrow, Bill."

On Thursday the *Mallard Cove Group*, as the new partnership was called, put the final touches on the documents they needed for the next day's closing. Kari, along with their lawyer, made sure that all their "t's" were crossed, and the "i's" dotted. Then late that afternoon three large boxes arrived full of long sleeve tee shirts with huge *Mallard Cove* logos on the back. Murph looked questioningly at Casey.

"Murph, hopefully we'll have a ton of crews showing up on Saturday, and we want them all leaving with a free shirt. It's the cheapest advertising there is. These will be popping up on docks and decks and showing up at tournaments throughout the mid-Atlantic and beyond. They'll be seen exactly where our potential customers are."

"Nice, Case, but it was just a surprise."

Casey nodded. "Told you we would handle the promotions. And this is one of Kari's ideas."

"Way to go, Kari!" Lindsay was impressed.

Kari smiled, pleased with the compliment. "Thanks. I ran the numbers, and it was cheaper to give everyone a shirt than it was to buy a one-month magazine ad in some of the regional magazines. Plus, these shirts and this logo will still be seen long after those magazines are rotting in some landfill."

Casey said, "I just hope we have enough people show up to make buying the shirts worthwhile."

Murph chuckled. "Case, you know better than to underestimate the power of free food and alcohol around the docks. Plus, we've got Baloney's mouth working overtime. He knows everybody, and most of 'em even listen to him. Trust me, there will be a crowd."

AT THE *BLUFFS* THAT EVENING, Betty Cooper did indeed turn out to be "a doll" just as Lindsay had said. She is about Bill's age and height, with salt and pepper shoulder-length hair. She also had a great laugh and smile that seemed to start up in her eyes and spread across her face. Best of all, Baloney was a bit quieter around her, giving everyone else a chance to talk. That included B2, who was the most outgoing Murph and Lindsay had ever seen him. His girlfriend Kim was a pretty brunette in her mid-twenties who was also outgoing and fun. The whole crew started with cocktails onboard *Predator.*

"Nice rig, Casey. Never been aboard a Jarrett Bay before." It impressed Baloney.

"Thanks, Bill. I fell in love with these boats the minute I saw them. This one is a fish-raising machine. She gets us out to the canyons fast and is a real stable platform once we get there. Pretty comfortable inside, too."

"I'll say! You two aren't going to be 'roughing it' at all this weekend. Nice!"

Casey smiled. "For a 'working weekend,' it should be fun. I'm hoping to get in some fishing on Sunday and see if we can find some migrating redfish by the beach on the way back. Oh, and speaking of work and fishing, we have a surprise for everyone at the barbeque."

They had already loaded the tee shirts aboard for the trip to *Mallard Cove*. Lindsay dug into the boxes and passed one out to each of the guests.

Baloney was impressed with the logo. "This is first class! Voorhees never even had a logo, an' he sure wasn't about ta spring for any shirts."

"And his marina is falling in and mostly empty, too." Murph was showing the grudge he was holding after his latest run-in with the man. "We've got a great team, and we're going to have that place full by this time next year. You're going to be turning down charters just so you can take a day off."

"That'd be nice. Voorhees sure hasn't done a thing ta help." Baloney had his own grudge.

"Well, that ends as of tomorrow. We're all in this together, Bill. If you're making money, it means we are, too. I don't think Voorhees understood that whole concept."

"He didn't, Murph. He was only interested in the part about the slip rent bein' on time. But now I don't have ta deal with him again, thanks ta you guys. An' you need ta know something that the gang all wanted me ta pass along. Everybody on that dock has got both yer backs, yers and Lindsay's too. We're all keepin' an eye out fer anybody acting suspicious around there now. They may have blown up your truck, but they took on alla us when they did that. So, when ya say we're all in this together, ya need to know we're already onboard, and not just the makin' money part."

Murph glanced at Lindsay, then nodded at Baloney. "Thanks, Bill, that means more than you know."

Casey jumped in. "Well, tonight is supposed to be fun and relaxing, so why don't we lighten it up, go take a look around at what we're doing here and then have some dinner."

They all climbed up on the dock. And relaxing evening or not, Dave was still on security duty, keeping watch. He followed them on their tour of the docks and into the restaurant, maintaining a quiet vigil. But his presence was a constant reminder that they couldn't completely drop their guard no matter where they went until they caught the bomber.

After dinner, Baloney was all smiles. "Murph and Lindsay, I gotta tell ya, I got worried when you guys told me ya were taking on partners instead ah just leasing out the restaurant. But after walking around here an' especially after that meal, I can see this was the smartest move ya coulda made. *Mallard Cove* will finally be what it shoulda been all along. After Saturday, the word's gonna be out about the new *Mallard Cove*, and I can't wait ta see the restaurant when it's finished. If the food there is half as good as here, you'll have a winner on your hands." Baloney had caught the same excitement that the partners all felt. In his mind he could already see what it was going to be like in a year. And he couldn't wait.

12

CLOSING TIME

Murph had been right about Voorhees. He was slightly hostile at the start of the closing but mellowed out once he had his check in hand. It was the only check he had ever seen with two commas on it, and it was payable to him. It was also enough money to ease his temper a bit. The two men even hesitantly shook hands after the deal, then they went their separate ways.

After the closing, Kari headed to *Mallard Cove* while Casey and Dawn dropped Murph and Lindsay back at *Bayside* then headed to the office. They would take *Predator* down to *Mallard Cove* later that afternoon. Murph and Lindsay boarded *Irish Luck* for their three-hour run down the opposite side of ESVA. That's when they discovered that Carlos had been aboard and had left them lunch as well as a basket of gourmet snacks. In the middle was a note congratulating them both on the closing and saying how he was looking forward to working with Murph again.

It touched Lindsay. "I like Carlos. He didn't need to do all that."

Murph said, "I'm not surprised, he's a good guy. I'm so glad he came up here with Casey and me. He's found his spot in the world where he can do what he wants, and work with the people he wants to be around. And we get to eat what he cooks. It's a win/win." He grinned. "And it hadn't really set in until I read his note, but together you and I now own the majority of a marina. How cool is that!"

Lindsay hugged him and had a huge smile. "First piece of real estate I've ever owned, and it should make money. You're good luck, you know that?"

"If I'm good luck, does that mean I'm gonna get lucky?" He had a mischievous grin.

"If you play your cards right, and if I get to run the boat down to the Cove."

"Deal! Crank 'em up, Captain, let's get going!"

The American checked the devices for the second time in two days. They were relatively simple as far as bombs go. No motion trigger, only a simple cell phone with a relay, a battery, and a blasting cap inserted into a C4 explosive. Each should have enough force to kill anyone within thirty meters. Where the one was going to be placed would mean that anyone within double that distance would be within range of the glass shrapnel. He smiled as he looked over at the cases of bottled beer that would multiply the number of casualties.

After this attack, the project will be as dead as anyone standing close to the bomb. And after buying the property, instead of removing the ways, he would add the railway that had already been designed to move the boats that were hauled. It would become a real boatyard, and all liveaboards would be banned from the docks. That way the *Grisham* could easily come and go with no prying eyes, no matter what time of night. He was also considering expanding his operation to include those wanting to covertly come into the country as well. His connections in the Mideast had brought up that possibility since they could send his containers back with more human cargo instead of empty. He was well aware of who those passengers would be; many of them were on the "*Do Not Fly*" list. As far as he was concerned, they were just more cargo that would have a very high price tag attached.

It all hinged on this one device working tomorrow, and since he was the one who built it and would be the one to place it, nothing was going to go wrong this time. If it did, he had the backup, just in case. But *Mallard Cove* should be as good as his.

Casey and Dawn waited to leave until mid-afternoon so they would arrive after quitting time. It was important that Murph, Lindsay, and Kari were the ones on site while the contractors were working. They wanted those three to form a close working relationship since the two of them wouldn't be down there as often. A little before three they pulled out of the *Bluffs* for what would only be a two-hour run for the much faster *Predator*.

Casey was at the helm as they passed through the inlet and into a very calm Atlantic Ocean. He said, "We haven't done this in a while, taken a boat ride all by ourselves."

Security for the barbeque, as well as coverage for Lindsay, Murph, Casey, and Dawn, was already scheduled for the rest of the weekend, or at least until they caught the bomber. Rikki had handled everything, and the security crew would already be waiting when they arrived at *Mallard Cove*. So, this boat trip was the only time that Casey and Dawn would be alone for the next two days or more.

"We need to do this more often and spend some time fishing with just the two of us." Dawn was next to Casey in the navigator's seat with her bare feet up on the console, looking very relaxed and content.

"You're right. Life isn't a dress rehearsal; you only get one shot at doing the things you love."

Dawn smiled and added, "With the ones you love." She paused a minute. "I'm proud of you."

"Why?"

"Doing this for Murph, Lindsay, and Kari. Setting them up in business."

Casey nodded. "Thanks, but they all needed this, and don't forget that we are still going to make money with this project too. Plus, I wouldn't have done it without you agreeing. If anybody should be proud of anyone else, it's me about you. Not too many people would forgive and forget as you did with Murph."

She laughed. "Don't kid yourself about that 'forget' part. You've heard the old saying, 'those that forget history are doomed to repeat it.' And I have always found that while it's good to forgive, it's smarter to never forget. I don't intend on making the same mistake twice, at least not in this lifetime."

Casey winced, thinking about his first two marriages. He had been taken in by two women he thought he knew, but as it turned out, he had been wrong about both. In each case, he had rushed into the marriages. Dawn understood that as well, and even though they were engaged, she wasn't pushing him about a wedding date. She knew he wasn't going anywhere, and neither was she. Life for the two of them was great together. She realized that this was the happiness they both hoped Lindsay and Murph would find, and she was glad that they were helping them discover a piece of the puzzle together with this project.

As *Irish Luck* cleared the breakwater and entered the marina basin a little after two in the afternoon, where it was obvious Kari had wasted no time in getting started. Their slip as well as those of the *Golden Dolphin, Kembe II,* and the empty slip just past theirs all had new pilings and had been both widened and lengthened. Now *Kembe II* would fit better in her slip, and *Predator* would fit nicely next to her for the weekend. When finished, the slips beyond that could also accommodate larger boats. The barge crew was already working on the fifth slip as a second crew replaced questionable planks on the dock. The first eight slips each had new shore power pedestals installed with integral dock lights. A big yellow grader was working in the parking area just beyond the dock as a line of dump trucks were taking turns dropping their crushed gravel loads.

Kari had spotted the Rybovich coming in and was already waiting on the dock along with Tony to catch their stern lines. "Hi, guys. We're making some good progress!"

Lindsay shut down the engines and said, "I'd say you're making *great* progress. No more having to dodge the truck-eating potholes on the way in, and these dock lights are going to be awesome at night. So, how can Murph and I help?"

"There's not much we can do today, other than watch. The crews all know their jobs. But take a walk with me and check out the new sign in the front. I had a front-end loader with a brush rake take out the scrub bushes so you not only can see the sign from the road, but now you can also see the restaurant and the marina, too. He's over stripping out the scrub from the old boatyard now, and it's really cleaning that area up."

Murph connected them to the shore power pedestal after he and Lindsay hopped up on the dock. All four headed toward the restaurant. A small skid loader was smoothing out new gravel where the captain's lounge was to be built and Kari had a tent coming for that area late today. The party was going to be set up in that same space the next day as they wanted to showcase the view from there.

As they continued toward the front of the property, Murph, and Lindsay were amazed at how well it could now be seen from the road. He commented, "Nothing will get the word out faster than people seeing progress without even having to get out of their cars. I didn't know you were doing all of this today."

Kari nodded. "I wanted to surprise you. I thought it was important to make a big visual statement about cleaning the place up. They're going to park the graders and equipment up here over the weekend so they can attract attention. People take notice of construction equipment."

They continued up to the temporary sign which was mounted high on two posts with solar-powered floodlights. It had the oval *Mallard Cove* logo with a sign underneath: "Under New Ownership – Marina Now Open – Charter Fishing Fleet" and under that was: "Restaurant Opening This Fall!"

Lindsay smiled at Kari. "That looks fantastic. I can't believe you've gotten this much done in less than a day. You being here is the best part of the whole deal; you're a wizard at this."

Kari beamed and blushed at the same time. "I'm just so thankful to own a small part of the project along with you guys. Casey had said that he would get me involved in some deals, but I didn't count on it. This was a great surprise for me, and it's a great feeling knowing that I'm helping build equity for all of us."

Murph said, "After sixteen years of both working with him and being his friend, take some advice from me. If Casey Shaw promises you something, you can 'take it to the bank.' Never cross him, and he'll always have your back. After our disagreement, most people would never have considered becoming partners together in anything again. But he's not most people, and I'm thankful he isn't." He turned and looked back at the restaurant and marina property. From where they stood they could see down the docks all the way to the *Grisham*. "You saw this from day one, didn't you, Kari?"

She nodded. "I did. And right now I can visualize the whole project finished, hotel and all."

Murph said, "You have the same gift as Casey. I started 'seeing it' from your drawings, and I get it even better now. But I know you both can see farther down the road than me."

Kari reminded him, "Yet you recognized the hidden value in the property, and without that, Cetta would own it now."

Murph said, "Lindsay, and I both did. And if she hadn't agreed to come in with me, I couldn't have afforded to commit to the deal." He smiled at Lindsay, who returned it.

THE AMERICAN WAS SO astonished that he almost drove off the road. He was returning from Virginia Beach with a brand-new cooler and had just gotten off the last bridge section of the CBBT when he saw the marina. Literally *saw it* from the highway, making him furious. Just hours before, the only thing that had been visible from here had been bushes and small trees that flanked a pockmarked old gravel access road. There hadn't even been a sign. But now there was a big one that touted the marina, charter fleet, and the soon-to-open restaurant. But what was even worse was that now he could easily see the *Grisham* as soon as he cleared the bridge. He hadn't figured on them moving this quickly, and it wasn't good. But after tomorrow night, it should stop all this in its tracks. It had better, or that year he put into planning the move will have been wasted. What had been done wasn't anything that eventually couldn't be undone by planting new bushes and trees, but in the meantime, they would have to be extra cautious.

"Holy crap, we're gonna have ta call you two the dynamic duo!" Baloney was backing the *Golden Dolphin* into his slip as B2 put the spring and bow lines on their new pilings. Murph jumped aboard and passed the stern lines to Lindsay up on the dock. Baloney looked at them both and said, "You two keep cleaning this place up, and we won't know how ta act." He wore a big grin.

Lindsay spoke up, "It was all Kari, she's overseeing the whole thing. We just picked the right partners. She's amazing." In just the three hours since they arrived, the tent for the party was erected, a construction trailer office had arrived and been placed, and was now powered up. The last gravel truck was preparing to drop its load, and the graders were about a half hour from being finished.

Bill and B2 helped their charter off the boat, then B2 took their catch to the cleaning table. Bill was a happy captain. "Ya don't know how great it is ta have new pilings. Last month when it was blowing so hard when I was backing inta the slip I had ta lay up against the starboard bow pile an' I hit it kinda hard. It made a big cracking sound, and I knew it wasn't gonna take much more ta break it in two. But Voorhees wasn't about ta replace it. Know what he said when I told him? 'So, just throw out your anchor on that side.' Ya believe the nerve of that guy?"

Murph laughed. "It's in the past, Baloney, so just forget it. Oh and wait until you see the road frontage now. They'll be able to see that Santa in your tuna tower from the fisherman inlet bridge!"

Just then they heard the *Kembe II*'s engines rumble as she cleared the breakwater, with *Predator* right behind her.

"Wow, rush hour at *Mallard Cove*. Who woulda thunk it?" Baloney was grinning as he said it.

AT THE BEER-THIRTY-BUNCH GATHERING, Murph had arrived at the patio before Hard Rock and Gaffer. He saw the pair coming up the dock and went out to intercept them. Baloney was standing next to Lindsay and said, "Uh, oh."

She shook her head and said, "If Gaffer is as sorry about running his mouth as you say, then he's got nothing to worry about from Murph."

They watched as Hard Rock tried to step between Gaffer and the approaching Murph. Then he and Murph had a short conversation, and Hard Rock reluctantly continued toward the patio, leaving the pair alone by themselves. Murph and Gaffer had a conversation that was more or less one-sided. Gaffer looked down and scuffed one foot back and forth while Murph talked. Gaffer nodded then looked up and said something as Murph stuck out his hand, which Gaffer took and shook. They both started toward the patio as the group inside let out a collective breath.

Baloney looked at Lindsay. "That's a good man ya got."

She nodded and smiled. "Don't I know it."

Casey and Dawn came in about thirty seconds after Murph and Gaffer. Off in the distance, they all saw Spud clearing the breakwater in his bait boat. This time as he tied up in front of the patio, there wasn't any noxious cloud following him.

Baloney asked him through the screen as he climbed out, "You gave her a real wash down?"

"Yeah, smartass, with bleach and everything. I figure I'll run her over here tomorrow afternoon, and I might even bring a date along, too."

The catcalls and whooping that followed prompted a single-digit response from Spud. He walked through the door and before he could ask, Murph threw him a can of Busch. "Thanks, Murph. Hey, this is starting to look like a real marina! I can't remember the last time I saw a barge in here fixing things."

Lindsay said, "You haven't seen anything yet. They're starting on the restaurant remodel this Monday. And before you guys gripe about losing the patio, the tent company is going to set up a small one over behind our boat when they pick up the one from the party. We'll still have a place to meet, rain or shine until the new captain's lounge is finished." They all applauded.

Baloney then launched into his story about Marlin Denton, and how they all needed to talk up the future of *Mallard Cove*. Lindsay asked why his nickname was "Shaker."

Before Bill could answer, Spud replied. "He jumped onto the covering board on the *Dolphin* a few years back, and his gut just kept jiggling. He used to carry a few extra pounds. So, smartass over there," he pointed at Baloney, "looks at him and says, 'Take it easy on the teak there, Shake-n-Bake!' Marlin went on a diet right after that and lost most of the extra weight. But once you're branded by Baloney, it's pretty much for life."

Lindsay looked at Jack Grayson. "Okay, I'm a little scared to ask how you got yours, Jack."

He looked sheepish. "Believe it or not, it didn't come from Bill. A few years back I decided to do a limited run of lithographs of one of my paintings I particularly liked. The best printers at the time were in Amsterdam. It's customary after they run the last print for the artist to destroy the plates, which are made of thin metal. They handed me a knife and indicated that I was to use it on the first plate. My Dutch was about as bad as the guy's English, so I took my cue from his gestures and did my best to cut the plate in two with the blade. He freaked out at first then started laughing. It turns out that you only have to scratch the plates to destroy them.

Well, they had a photographer there who took pictures of the whole thing. The next day the local paper had my picture on the front page with the caption in Dutch, 'Jack the Ripper.' I was staying at a hotel owned by an American friend, and he made sure the story along with several copies of the paper got back to our mutual friends in the States, including Bill."

"Yeah, and do ya think that cheapskate over here would give me one of those prints? Hell no!" Baloney was disgusted.

"Bill, you live aboard the *Golden Dolphin*. The lithographs are large, and you don't have any place to even hang one." Jack furrowed his brow as he said it.

"I don't want ta hang one of the damned things, I'd wanna sell it!" Baloney almost looked serious.

Casey glanced at Dawn, who nodded as she silently laughed. They knew for sure that Murph and Lindsay were right in wanting to build the captain's lounge to keep the camaraderie going. It was stories that were told in groups like this that separated marinas like *Mallard Cove* from the more sterile feeling, corporate-run ones. They were hoping the same atmosphere would emerge soon over at the *Bluffs*. They understood that all it took was a nucleus, and in this case that was a loud but well-meaning New Jersey native nicknamed Baloney.

13

TIME TO GO

Marlin Denton pulled up to the bulkhead in front of the *Golden Dolphin* in *Bone Shaker*, his eighteen-foot Maverick flats boat, shortly before ten on Saturday morning. Baloney was already waiting for him.

"Shaker, what took ya so long? I thought ya would be here hours ago!"

"You said to meet you here on Saturday morning Baloney, and it'll be morning for another two hours, so I'm not late. Hey, new pilings?" He motioned toward the *Dolphin's* bow.

"That's part ah what I wanted ta show you. They put 'em in while I was out fishin' yesterday. I told ya these kids are serious about fixin' the place up. An' this is only temporary 'til they get through all the government red tape ta replace it all with floatin' docks. C'mon with me, and I'll introduce ya around."

An hour later Shaker had met Murph, Lindsay, Casey, and Dawn, and seen the plans for what was going to happen. He was almost as excited as Baloney and happy about the idea of moving there. He and Bill came out of the construction trailer, which was also serving as a temporary office until they built a new one next to the captain's lounge. Marlin was officially the first to sign a slip rental agreement with the new owners, and he had actually signed three.

Baloney said, "Yer gonna love it here, Marlin. An' while ya already got a big client list, once everything is up and runnin', I think you're gonna add to it real easy. This place is gonna be a big draw."

"I had no idea all this was going to happen. Now I'm glad that Cetta raised my rent, he can stick it."

"I told ya I'd get ya a good deal," Baloney bragged.

"Bill, you never said a word about that in there. How did *you* get me a good deal?"

"I softened 'em up for ya yesterday. It was all in the works before we even went through the door. Ya can thank me now, Shaker!"

Marlin shook his head, obviously recognizing a "Baloney-ism" when he heard it but decided to cover the bases, anyway. "Thanks... Baloney." He used Bill's nickname in a way that could be taken either as gratitude or scorn then followed it with a sly smile.

"Yeah, well, yer welcome. Let's go check out what they're cookin'." Baloney led the way over to where three large trailer-mounted charcoal cookers loaded with ribs, brisket, and chicken was being tended by a chef. Next, they walked over under the tent. "So, this is gonna be the view from our lounge. We get a pretty good crowd here in the afternoons. But th' patio is goin' back to being part of the restaurant. They had me come up ta the *Bluffs* ta try out the food. It was unbelievable, so they should pack this place alla the time. You'll see what I'm talkin' about with the food this afternoon, they know what they're doing."

Baloney then led Shaker over onto the patio to look in the windows of the restaurant. "Alla these people are gonna have a great view of us when we come in, an' the new lighted fish cleaning tables will be right out there in front. Every one ah their restaurant customers is a potential charter customer of ours, and they'll have a front-row seat as we come in. I'm telling you, this'll be great!"

Marlin said, "Bill, I already signed the contract. You don't have to sell me anymore."

"I'm not sellin', I'm excited for the both of us! Oh, hey, Murph brought his beer cooler back. Maybe he loaded it up again." He walked over to where the cooler sat against the textured plywood knee wall that butted up next to the tent. "Bingo! Hey, Shaker, let's have a beer to celebrate your moving here."

"Baloney, it's not even noon yet."

"Well, it's close enough. An' today is supposed to be about havin' fun and showing everyone a good time. All I'm suggestin' is we get a head start." Bill grabbed a Heineken as Marlin spotted his favorite Mexican beer. He pulled one from the ice which had frozen together, leaving a perfectly round, bottle-shaped hole in the surrounding ice. He looked down and saw the top of a food storage container at the bottom. Thinking it might be full of lime wedges, he dug through the ice. When he recognized what was behind the now exposed clear top, he jumped back.

"Whoa! Let's get out of here, Bill, there's a bomb in there!"

"What? Where?" He peered in then backed up. "We need ta go tell Murph!"

Marlin was reaching for his phone. "We need to call the cops!"

Bill grabbed his arm. "Don't use that in here, we ain't sure what might set it off. Murph has some security people around that are workin' with the cops and they'll know how to handle it." The two of them hurried down the dock and spotted Murph and Lindsay talking to Rikki Jenkins, who had pulled up a minute before with a half dozen more of her security crew.

Bill raced up to Murph. "There's a bomb in your cooler, Murph!"

"What cooler? That one?" Murph pointed to the cooler that he used the other day, which was sitting on the dock.

"No, your cooler up on the patio. At least I thought it was yours, it looked just like it. Anyway, there's a bomb in the bottom in a food container."

Rikki addressed Bill. "How do you know it's a bomb? Can you describe it?"

"It's one ah those clear top food containers like you'd have in a 'fridge. There's a cell phone in it sittin' on a buncha clay-looking stuff, and some wires. If it ain't a bomb, it's a damned good imitation."

"You're sure it has a cell phone with it."

"Yeah, it's one ah those cheap ones like you can get in a convenience store. Who the heck are you?"

Murph answered, "This is Rikki, and she is in charge of security for the party and us. She'll handle this."

Rikki nodded at Murph. "Right. And the first thing we need to do is get you back into your boat. In fact, all of you need to get on board, and don't mention this to anyone." She turned to one of the group she had brought with her. "Mike, grab some gloves and a laptop-sized Faraday bag out of my truck. Let's check this thing out, and if there's no motion switch, maybe we can bag it." The man nodded, then retrieved a large black nylon bag from the truck. He and Rikki headed down the dock in the direction of the patio while Murph, Lindsay, Bill, and Marlin went into the cabin on *Irish Luck*.

Mike had been in Explosive Ordinance Disposal while in the Navy. One glance told him that it was an active bomb.

"Rikki, get the hell out of here."

"What are you going to do?"

"Separate that phone and blasting cap from the plastique. Doesn't look like there's any trip or motion switch, and I doubt whoever built this wants to blow up an empty patio. It's probably for later when there's a crowd around under the tent. Now get out of here and let me get to work."

Five minutes later he walked out with the Faraday bag and the container. "We're good. I bagged the phone so it can't get any signal. Now we can back off and watch the place to see if anyone comes to check it. But I doubt that if I tried to set it off and it didn't work, that I'd want to stick my head back in there. Judging by the amount of ice melt, I'd guess that whoever planted it must have done it last night. Even around a dock, during daylight hours people tend to notice someone with a big cooler."

Rikki nodded. "I agree, they probably would have placed it when there wasn't anyone else around. We can get the number off the phone and see who calls it, and from where. Chances are it was the same guy that blew up Casey's plane. Cell phone, plastic explosive, meaning the same type of construction. He'll probably want to be within sight of the tent when he sets it off, but far enough away to be clear of the blast zone." She called Sheriff Roberts and reported what they found, and what they had done. He wasn't happy.

"You should have called me first and cleared out of there! You could have been blown to shreds, not to mention contaminating the evidence."

Rikki was irritated. "My EOD expert had four tours in Iraq and Afghanistan and has disarmed more live bombs than any of the State Police or your guys have ever seen or practiced with. Whoever set this up is an amateur. But I guarantee he's close by, and if he'd seen a bunch of your cars roll in here, he probably would have set it off early just to destroy the evidence." She told him about her plan to get the number off the phone and track whoever called it. The sheriff calmed down as she explained.

"Well, that makes sense. But that cooler is evidence as well as the bomb, and I don't want it touched."

Rikki rolled her eyes. "The bomb is the best evidence, and it can be concealed when I put it in a car and bring it to you. If you try to take that cooler out of the patio I guarantee the bomber will see you and spook. So long as it stays put, he'll think he's safe and we can catch him."

The sheriff had to concede the point. "Okay. But I'm putting a team of my deputies down there with your group."

"So long as they are dressed in shorts and fishing shirts they won't draw any attention. Nobody knows how many crews or owners are going to show up anyway, so a bunch of unfamiliar faces won't be suspicious."

"Exactly. Now meet me at the gas station a half mile north of there, and we'll take custody of that device. I'll need your EOD guy to come with me and make a statement."

"We're heading out now."

. . .

RIKKI RETURNED twenty minutes later and went straight to *Irish Luck*. She found that Casey and Dawn had joined the group inside.

"I dropped Mike off with the sheriff. He'll catch a ride back with some of the plain-clothes deputies." She looked at Marlin. "You look a little shaken up still."

He angrily replied, "Murph just told me about everything. I had heard about his truck, but not the plane. How can you even think about having a party here now? That bomb wasn't put there just for Murph and Lindsay, it was to kill a bunch of people under that tent! You've got to cancel it."

Rikki shook her head. "First, we would never intentionally put anyone else at risk. My people are the best in the business, and we would have discovered that bomb not long after you did. I have over a dozen operatives here as well as a bomb dog and they had just started searching the area. They're careful not to be obvious about it because we know the bomber is likely to be somewhere close by once the party starts. This is our best shot at catching him now that we're sure the target is the crowd itself. The sheriff will be waiting for the call to that phone, so then we can pinpoint the caller's location."

Marlin wasn't convinced. "He could be anywhere. Even in the woods, or on a boat offshore."

Rikki nodded. "He could, but we would see him. We'll have our drones up with infrared systems that will patrol the perimeter including the woods, water, and even the parking area. Believe me, we have this covered. This kind of work is what we specialize in."

"Then how come I've never heard of you?"

"Because you've never needed to, and we're good. If we had ever screwed up, believe me, you would have heard of us. But I've got a long list of very satisfied customers."

Casey said, "And I'm one of them. Our resort, *Chesapeake Bayside*, has a lot of high-profile guests. It's also one of the most secure resorts anywhere, yet you won't notice anything or anyone obvious about it. All our security is handled by Rikki's firm. Trust me, they're the best in the business. So you are as secure here, right now, as you would be even over there. You have my word on that."

Murph saw that Marlin still wasn't convinced. He said, "Rikki's people had already planned to sweep this place several times, so I guarantee there won't be any surprises. But I'll tell you what, Marlin, let's go over to the office and tear up those contracts, and you can be on your way. I'm not going to force you into anything you aren't comfortable with. I do want you to know though that I'd never put anyone at risk over business. I'm comfortable with Rikki's plan. I would appreciate you keeping this to yourself though." He stood up, waiting for Marlin to do the same.

Marlin remained in his seat. "Baloney, are you going to tell me that you aren't worried?"

"I was worried 'till we got the hell away from that thing. But if Murph, Big Tuna, Dawn, and Lindsay aren't scared ta be here, then neither am I. Dammit, Shaker, this marina has been my home for the last ten years. I've watched as it went ta hell 'cause Voorhees was too cheap ta fix anything. Still somehow, I made a livin' off this dock. Now we've finally got people who give a damn about this place, and I know my bookings are gonna get better because of it. But for some reason, it looks like someone wants ta scare us out of here. Well, he's not gonna chase me off. Hey, Rikki, you guarantee it's gonna be safe tonight?"

"Absolutely, Bill."

"That's good enough for me. No pissant coward with a cell phone trigger is gonna run me outa here. The bastard doesn't even have the balls ta do this face to face. When ya think about it, a bomber is about as big a coward as they come. By staying here tonight, this says I'm braver than he is. So, yeah, I'm telling you I'm not worried, Shaker. You do whatcha want, but I'm stayin' ta help these kids build a business, and defend the one that I've built too. This is the best location on the Shore for a charter fleet, and it's gonna get even better. But if this shindig gets canceled or word gets out and people stay away, I'll have ta move and start over from scratch. Not many places around with an empty slip on a charter dock, 'specially the prime slip. So, if we keep what we found out just ta this group, then everything'll be fine. When that bastard calls that number and the cops catch him, it won't matter anymore, anyway."

Shaker looked directly into Rikki's eyes. What he saw was the determination and confidence of someone who was the best at what she did, and she didn't blink or look away. But he didn't know her, and he wasn't about to trust his life to a stranger, no matter what Bill said.

"Murph, I don't want to rip up those contracts because I'd still like to move my boats over here. But I just don't know about being at the barbeque today since we know it was a target. I think I'll wait until your bomber gets caught before I move over here, too."

"I understand, and that's fine. But please keep what happened under wraps, okay? If word gets out, we might not be able to catch this guy." Murph was worried, not just about the bomber, but at the idea that Marlin might say something to someone who might spread the word. If they didn't have a big turnout because people stayed away out of fear, the bomber would get exactly what he wanted just as if he had detonated the device.

Marlin nodded and got up. "I'll keep it to myself." He looked over at Baloney, who was disappointed to see Shaker leaving. "See you later, Bill."

Baloney looked away. "Yeah whatever, Shaker." He had been looking forward to him being not just at the barbeque but becoming part of their afternoon group. Now he wasn't so sure he wanted him to join them.

TWO HOURS LATER, Baloney's cell phone rang. He was surprised to see who the caller was. "Whatta ya want, Marlin?"

Marlin winced because he knew Baloney only used his given name when he was mad. "I'm on my way back, about five minutes out. I'm by myself on my Chris Craft, dragging my flats boat. Can you give me a hand tying up?"

Baloney was caught off guard not expecting Marlin to change his mind, especially not so quickly. He hesitated at first then said, "Okay, meet me at the gas dock."

Five minutes later Baloney jumped on the flats boat and ran it over to its new slip a couple of spots down from Murph. Then he climbed aboard Shaker's vintage forty-two-foot Chris Craft Constellation as he backed her into the adjacent slip. After they got her tied up and the shore power switched on, Shaker grabbed a couple of beers from the galley refrigerator. They sat down in a pair of director's chairs on the back deck.

"Why'd you come back, Shaker?"

"I was on my way over to Lynnhaven when that Kenny Chesney song 'Boston' came on the stereo. I remembered that he said he'd only play that in New England as a tribute to them all being 'Boston Strong.' It was in honor of the survivors of the marathon bombings, and also those who came back to watch the next year. Everybody there that day a year later knew they had a target on their backs, but they trusted the experts to get it right and keep them safe. They also knew that by staying away they would let the bastards win. And I'm not going to help this guy win either, it's not who I am."

Baloney reached out and tilted his bottle as Shaker met it with his. "I'm glad you changed your mind. They'll catch this guy, then we can all relax. Meanwhile, we've got ah couple ah hours until this shindig starts. Do you want a ride over to pick up your truck? I can probably get Betty to drive us, then you can bring back your Gold Line, too."

"Let's go."

14

REDIAL

An hour and a half later Shaker's last boat was tied up, and they had unloaded his bait freezer and dock boxes. Just as they finished, Murph showed up.

"Great timing there, Murph. I only wrenched my back getting that freezer offa his truck with only him an me." Baloney whined.

"Well, Baloney, I'll buy you a beer. You can hold it on your back or drink it. Your call." Murph turned to Shaker and held out some papers. "Here's some updated contracts that you need to sign. These include free dockage for all three boats through next month. Lindsay and I wanted you to know that we appreciated you coming back today."

"Thanks, Murph, but you didn't need to do that."

"Yeah, Murph, you didn't need ta do that for Shaker. But you can do that for me!" Baloney was back in form.

Murph smiled and pulled another contract from his back pocket. "Here you are, Bill. Same terms as Marlin's, three years locked in at your current rate with a five percent maximum annual cap for any increases after that. Sign here on the dotted line."

"Thanks, Murph. And *two* months free dockage, right?"

"Uh, okay." He took out a pen and grinned as he opened the paper.

Baloney got a questioning look on his face, "Hey wait a minute, you caved too easy. What gives?"

"Well, I'll change it to two months as you wanted. Though I had made it three since you brought in Marlin's three boats. I was thinking of a free month for each annual contract but in this case two works fine. Plus, I was going to make that a continuous offer of a free month's rent for any additional annual slip renters you two sign up."

Baloney snatched the papers from Murph's hand before he could change it. "Never mind, three works, and we'll drag 'em in, kickin' and screamin' if we have ta! You got a pen?"

Murph handed him his pen with a chuckle. "By the way, we gave you guys a break on the rates too. Because we're counting on you to talk it up and help fill this place as we get it ready."

Shaker said, "You won't have any problem with that, especially when the hotel and bars are finished. But I think I might be able to talk a few into joining us in the meantime."

Murph smiled, knowing he had picked the right two for help.

Rikki's group blended in well with the partygoers who began arriving around four. Some of the sheriff's deputies were easier to spot, however, with their untanned legs that came from wearing their long pants while on duty. Rikki hoped the bomber wouldn't notice that just as she had, or maybe he'd figure they were non-boating free-loaders. She saw Murph and Casey each had a beer, and were sitting at one of the two dozen tables that were set up under the tent. They looked up as she approached, and Murph indicated the chair next to his. He faced her as she sat down.

"Everything good?"

Rikki nodded. "So far. My crew works around boats enough to make any conversation easy, so they're fitting right in. Some of the deputies, well, not so much."

"Yeah, I noticed. They're the only suspicious ones I've seen so far, and they're on our side."

Rikki gave him a slight grin as she watched an attractive young woman in shorts and a loose-fitting vented fishing shirt chatting up two guys dressed in similar clothes. She held the leash of a large male chocolate Labrador retriever who sniffed each man in turn before she pulled him back.

Murph followed her gaze. "What? Does she look suspicious to you?"

Rikki shook her head. "No. She's with us, and Tide has one of the best noses for explosives I've ever seen. Smart as a whip, too. See how he checked out each of those guys without raising any suspicion? Looked like he was an overly friendly pup. You can't teach that, it's pure canine genius. I haven't seen too many that are at his level."

"I've always loved dogs, and Tide is now high on my list of favorites." Murph had more than a touch of admiration in his voice.

Casey and Murph kept watching as Tide and his handler continued working the crowd, targeting mainly males. Rikki explained, "Nobody is off the list of potential suspects. But statistically speaking, going by the history of past remote bombers, the odds are our guy is a male. But because we don't have a really clear motive yet, we can't depend solely on that. Though I have a gut feeling that's right, and that he's close by. Tide's not only searching for devices, but for any explosive residue that might be on someone's hands or clothes. But we also have several hidden cameras which are recording all of the crowd for later analysis. We'll run it through facial recognition and see if we catch our boy if he has a record."

"Hey, Murph, you need ta meet my buddy, 'Cigar Louie'." Baloney had a live one chummed up. "He's got a thirty-six Luhrs ah few miles North, an' I was telling him how great it is being here on the southern point ah the Shore. Take a left, an' you're headed to the canyons, or ah right puts ya out in the bay. Now you need ta tell him what ya got planned."

Murph put on his sales hat and got up to give 'Cigar Louie' the dog and pony show. As he did, Dawn and Lindsay walked up. Murph beckoned to Lindsay while Dawn split off and took the seat that he'd vacated between Casey and Rikki.

"So far, so good. Seems to be a lot of interest in what's going to happen here and not just in the free food." Dawn was pleased. "Are you going to go help Murph and Lindsay?"

Casey shook his head. "Nope, it's their baby, and nobody is better equipped to sell it than those two. Plus, Bill and Marlin are both working the crowd. This works: Bill is outgoing and appeals to a certain crowd while Marlin is more laid back, which appeals to the rest. Murph's idea of the dockage credit for any contracts the two of them bring in was great, they're really trying."

"Speaking of trying, I've got to get back to doing my part. I'll check with you soon." Rikki got up and left.

Dawn said, "Casey, wait until you see what's next. Lindsay's been working with Kari on the social media pages. She and Murph are going to do videos that will get broadcast live and then edited and uploaded to those pages. They are going to do interviews with as many of the prospective customers as they can. Most of them have their own pages, especially the charter boat crews, so these are going to be shared all across the internet. See, she's already doing one with Baloney, Murph, and that 'Cigar Louie' fellow."

It impressed Casey. "I never thought to do any of that. Heck, I don't even have any social media accounts. Then again, I don't want any, either."

"Actually, we have them for the restaurants. So, in a way, you do. Remind me when we are back in the office to show you. Kari manages them."

"I've kind of lost touch with things like that. I've been so busy with the overall picture of things." Casey almost sounded disappointed.

"You are focusing where we need you to. You lead, and we'll take care of the details. It works. I guarantee that Murph didn't know about the interviews until now, either. But it looks like he's having fun with it." Dawn was right, Murph loved the camera, and they could see Baloney and Louie soaking up the attention. This was going to be great advertising, and it was all for free.

THE AMERICAN COULDN'T BELIEVE his luck. Not only was the tent area filling up fast as people claimed tables for themselves and their friends, but Lindsay and Murph were doing live social media broadcasts. He watched on his smartphone as the number of watchers steadily increased as the interviewees "liked" the marina's page and shared it before their interviews. This meant that he was going to be able to be completely away from the blast area and still watch the results up close in real-time. He had planned to detonate the device right after dark, but now he decided to move his schedule up to when there was still plenty of daylight. He wanted to make sure that they could capture the explosion clearly, and that the video of it would go viral. This was perfect.

THE BAND that had been hired played a mix of island songs, yacht rock, and new country. A portable wooden dance floor had been set up in front of the rented bandstand. Soon it had a crowd that overflowed out into the Astroturf beyond it. Spud was in the middle, putting on a show for the pretty blonde he had shown up with. Ripper and his wife Carol were on the edge, moving nicely to the beat. Murph opened the camera app and panned from the band to the dance crowd while giving a short narrative, mostly letting the scene tell the story. It said this place was happening, and this was the vibe that they intended to keep going when the restaurant's new bar opened.

OVER BY THE part of the boatyard that had yet to be cleared of scrub, the American pressed the send button on the burner phone as he simultaneously watched the dancing scene on his smartphone. The expected flash and carnage never came. He hung up the burner, checked the number, and pressed send again. Nothing. Suddenly it hit him just how bad things might have gone. He walked out onto the end of the finger pier on the side of the ways as he broke the burner apart. He stealthily dropped pieces into the water as he walked from there back across the yet-to-be-repaired section of the docks. Then he removed his disposable nitrile gloves and tossed them into the trash barrel where a small pile already lay at the bottom. This was a common sight in boatyards, and the crew that had painted the bottom of the last boat that launched off the ways two days ago had used those other blue gloves. Then he returned to the tent which he had left only five minutes before.

Sheriff Roberts answered his phone and signaled his deputies, then led them to the parking area where they split up. Half went to watch for people running for their car, and the others went to watch for any boat that might try to make a getaway. Begrudgingly he texted Rikki's phone, letting her know that someone had called the bomb trigger phone twice. They had triangulated the position of the caller, and it had shown up as having come from the marina property. Additional efforts to ping the phone's present location had proved futile, and they assumed the phone's battery had already been removed.

While they were watching for someone leaving in a hurry, additional cars, and a few boats were still arriving. They paid no attention as a car drove in and continued down the boatyard's driveway and out to the *Grisham*. However, the new arrival wasn't lost on the American as it passed him. He had spotted Volkan, Elif, and the girl from New Jersey in the car. At first, he was furious that the girl was still alive, but then quickly realized that the only reason they would have fled the farm and come here was that things had gone terribly, terribly wrong, like his planned explosion had. He joined the crowd in the tent, making his way toward the dance floor. He didn't dare approach the patio or look through the screen to see if the cooler was still in place. But he had been keeping an eye out all day for the cooler. He was sure that if they had discovered it, there would have been a swarm of police or at least the bomb squad. His mind was racing. He wanted to run down to the *Grisham* to find out what happened but knew that it would look suspicious. His standing orders were that in case of trouble they were to destroy their phones before they left the farm property and get to the *Grisham*. Those phone pieces should now be in the ditch alongside the main road leading to the marina.

The American would make his way to the *Grisham* later after things died down. The original plan was that they would all escape on that big steel research vessel. But now he was switching to his "Plan B," and they would all have a part to play in it.

THE SHERIFF CAME over to where Rikki was now standing with Murph and Lindsay. "There've been some new developments. Someone saw a couple of runaway girls being abducted from the Virginia Beach bus depot by a man and a woman that fit the description of the mall shooters. They were also spotted this time as they switched vehicles. The witness was able to get a description and plate number. The registration's address was a farm about ten miles from here. FBI's ACTeam stormed the place and found the two abducted girls safe, but the abductors must have somehow known they were coming and had already fled. They also found your bomber's workshop there. So, chances are that he's as slippery as his accomplices. He probably got away before we started checking cars and boats that were leaving. The ACTeam thinks they are all heading north, back toward New Jersey where they might have contacts that can help hide them. I'm taking my deputies over there to help with the investigation, and we'll take that bomb cooler along with us. You should be safe here now since they're all on the run."

After the sheriff left, Murph asked Rikki, "You think he's right?"

She answered, "You don't see me pulling my team just yet, do you? So long as this party is happening we're going to keep our guard up, just in case. Better safe than sorry. If we get past this without any incident, then I might start to relax. But only then."

. . .

Several hours later the band, Carlos's crew, all the invited partygoers, and Rikki's team had all packed up and left. There hadn't been any further incidents. Murph, Lindsay, Casey, Dawn, Shaker, and Baloney were now sitting around a table under the tent after liberating a cooler of leftover beer and wine.

"Hey, it looks like I won't be writing you guys a check anytime soon! Three more annual contracts mean I don't pay rent for half a year now." Baloney was grinning from ear to ear with his usual unlit cigar now perched in the corner of his mouth.

Murph replied, "Yep, and Marlin nailed two more than you did."

"No! How the hell did you pull that off, Shaker?"

"Simple. I let them do most of the talking, Baloney. They couldn't get a word in edge-wise with you!" Everyone else at the table joined Marlin in a good laugh except Bill, whose cigar moved from one corner of his mouth to the other by itself in a show of aggravation.

"Yeah, well, I gave ya all the easy marks. I had ta work for mine, so I should get double the free rent," he griped.

Lindsay smiled, "Nice try, Bill. But seriously, we are grateful that you guys helped us get a nice jumpstart toward increasing the charter fleet and adding some private boats as slip renters. Not too shabby for only owning the place for two days."

Baloney nodded. "That's more boats than Voorhees ever added in the last two years! An' I know there are a lot more out there that are just waiting ta see what happens with the restaurant. But I can tell ya, the food was a huge hit. Especially those sea cake sandwich thingies. Your guy knows what he's doing. And as soon as the hotel goes up with the pool, the second restaurant, and bar, that'll be a big draw."

"Well, I hate to part good company, but I'm beat." Lindsay stood and stretched.

Bill said, "Yeah, Betty hit the bunk a little while ago, and I've got an afternoon half day tomorrow, so I'll walk over with you."

Murph looked at her, "I just started this beer, but I'll be right behind you after it's gone."

"Take your time, babe, I'm just going to check the media page on the computer, then zonk out." She started toward the dock with Baloney next to her.

After those two left, Marlin said, "You know, four of my sign-ups were from Cetta-owned marinas, and at least one of Bill's was. You couldn't have timed this better with him just having raised all of his rents. He's going to be so pissed!" After getting hit by Cetta's new rates Marlin loved getting some payback.

Murph grinned. "I wonder if it still hurts for him to sit down?" The others chuckled, having seen it happen or heard the story. "That man is going to hate me even more than he does now!"

LINDSAY SAID goodnight to Baloney as he stepped aboard the *Golden Dolphin*. She continued down the dock and was just coming up on the *Irish Luck* when she spotted a couple of shadowy figures in the dark area down by the ways. She decided to check them out because something just didn't feel right about the two. They were beyond the part with the new dock lights and were only silhouetted by a single mercury vapor lamp that was beyond them, over next to the *Grisham*. She reached around to make sure her Glock nine-millimeter was still in her back holster. After reassuring herself that it was, she continued walking toward them as they stopped and stood still. She was about twenty feet away when she recognized the man, and a split second later she realized that the woman was actually the teenager from the mall that had been with the Turkish couple. What was she doing here with... Suddenly Lindsay felt something hit her in the chest as the world went blindingly white. She realized she was falling, but couldn't stop herself, and everything changed to black as her head hit the dock.

15

SAYING GOODBYE HURTS

Murph walked down the dock and noticed in the distance that the *Grisham's* running lights were on, and she was pulling away from the bulkhead. He didn't think that much of it, because she departed and arrived at weird hours; this wasn't all that uncommon for research vessels. He stepped onto *Irish Luck* and went into the salon. Murph saw that Lindsay's tablet and laptop were both still on the galley counter where she had left them earlier. He went down the stairs and into their stateroom, but Lindsay wasn't there. He checked the forward stateroom and the head, but she wasn't in either. Suddenly, he was filled with a deep dread. Racing out into the cockpit, he looked up at the flybridge which was vacant, then he checked the foredeck, which was also empty. Casey and Dawn were coming down the dock, headed toward *Predator*.

"Hey! Did you guys see Lindsay?"

Dawn answered, "No. She isn't onboard?"

"No! She said she was coming down here, twenty minutes ago."

The only other lights on any of the boats came from the cabin of Marlin's Chris Craft. The trio headed over there where Murph called out, "Lindsay? Are you onboard?"

Marlin came up on his back deck from the cabin. "What's going on?"

Murph answered, "Is Lindsay with you?"

"Lindsay? No. I thought she was going back to your boat." Marlin sounded confused.

"She was, but she's not there."

Dawn asked, "Have you tried her phone?"

"No. Good idea." Murph tried her number which rang until it finally switched to voicemail. "No answer."

Marlin asked, "Does she have that 'Find My Phone' app on her tablet?"

Murph snapped his fingers. "Yes! Why didn't I think of that?"

All four raced over to *Irish Luck* and Murph fired up the tablet. "What the heck? This shows that her phone is out on the water and moving slowly south!"

Dawn asked, "Whose boat would she have gotten on?"

Murph replied, "Nobody's! At least, not willingly. And the only boat I know that left here in the last hour was the *Grisham*. That's gotta be it, she's onboard the *Grisham*! Somebody on that tub took her. We've got to go get her back!"

Marlin volunteered, "We can take my Gold Line, she's the fastest boat in here."

Murph replied, "Let's go! She'd have never left on her own, somebody grabbed her. You have a gun, Marlin?" Because of the bomber, Murph, Casey, and Dawn were all carrying theirs.

"Yes, I'll get it. But you need to call the sheriff, too."

"We've got no time to wait! Every second counts, she's getting farther and farther away. We have to go now! We can call the sheriff from out on the water." Murph was close to panicking.

Marlin grabbed his stainless steel .357 magnum Smith & Wesson revolver and his boat keys from the cabin then he hopped aboard *Marlinspike,* followed by all the others. He started the twin 200-horsepower Mercury outboards as the others threw off the lines. The boat was already up on a plane and still accelerating before they even left the basin. According to Lindsay's tablet, the *Grisham* had about a five-nautical-mile lead on them and looked to be running about fifteen knots. With the Gold Line moving at thirty-five knots, Marlin figured they should catch up with the old research vessel in about fifteen minutes.

MURPH REACHED SHERIFF ROBERTS, who told him to stop and wait for the Coast Guard. He said he was going to get them to intercept the *Grisham*. Murph was in front of the center console and still almost had to yell to be heard over the sound of the wind and the screaming engines. He didn't bother arguing, he simply hung up. Murph turned to his three friends and yelled, "I can't believe that guy. He wanted us to wait for the 'Coasties'. No way I'm doing that! She could be all the way to North Carolina before they ever catch up to her."

"I've got them on the radar, three miles ahead. We'll be on them in less than ten minutes." Marlin yelled back at Murph.

Five minutes later the lights of the *Grisham* came into view, a mile, and a half ahead. Suddenly there was a huge flash and a mushrooming column of fire arose from the area where the *Grisham*'s lights had appeared. The locator dot on the tablet disappeared, as Murph let out an anguished, "Noooooo! Lindsay!"

BACK AT *MALLARD COVE*, the American was standing on the rip-rap breakwater over on the commercial side. Even from eight miles away, on this moonless night, he had seen the flash of fire out on the ocean and knew that at least this last device had worked correctly. All of those loose ends were now tied up. No accomplices left to rat him out to the Feds in exchange for lighter sentences. They had gotten too reckless, and it had been getting worse instead of better. There were plenty of others that would be happy to take their places for what he was willing to pay. He smiled as he broke apart yet another phone and tossed the pieces into the water. Then he turned and walked back down the wharf toward the boatyard, disappearing into the darkness beyond the reach of the single dock light.

~

Two minutes later *Marlinspike* pulled up next to the slick that had come from the *Grisham*. Some of the diesel fuel and engine oil were still on fire on the surface, slowly being fed by what was left of the tanks and drums on the wreck, now thirty feet beneath the surface.

"Lindsaaaaay! Lindsaaay! Where are you?" Murph was screaming at the top of his lungs from the bow, but the only other sound came from Marlin's idling outboards.

Marlin used a handheld spotlight to scan the area, but there was no one left alive from the boat. Most of the debris that was floating was badly burned. His light hit what they thought was a log until they realized it was part of a body that had been ripped apart by the initial blast and burned before the wreckage sank. That's when the full realization of the situation hit Murph, no one on board could have survived that huge explosion. Lindsay was gone. He half-sat, half fell onto the console's front seat with a vacant expression on his face. Casey came up and sat beside him while Dawn stood next to Murph and put an arm across his shoulders as she softly cried for her lost friend.

Half an hour later two Coast Guard patrol boats were sweeping the area as Marlin stood by, his boat just outside of the floating debris trail. He had passed along the GPS coordinates of the wreck since the current and the slight breeze had now carried most of the debris quite a distance from the site of the explosion. Two officers had boarded Marlin's boat, taking all their statements. One addressed Marlin, "You probably need to get Captain Murphy home. He looks like he's in shock, and there's nothing more any of you can do out here. We'll be in touch if we need more information, Captain Denton. We'll also coordinate with the sheriff's office and their land-based investigation."

"Right. Thanks for your help." Marlin ran the two officers over to their vessel. He then set a course back to *Mallard Cove* at a slower and much quieter cruising speed. Casey rode up front next to Murph while Dawn sat on the lean seat with Marlin.

"It could be that she wasn't on that boat when it exploded." Dawn looked hopefully at Marlin. "I mean, nobody saw her get onboard. Or maybe she jumped overboard somewhere between there and the marina, and she's swimming toward shore now."

Marlin didn't want to crush her hopes, but he also wanted to be realistic about things. "Dawn, we were chasing her phone signal, and it quit at the same time as the explosion. Do you think it's likely that she left it onboard? Did she lose it often?"

She looked down. "I've only known her a few months, but I've never seen her without it."

"We were right there just minutes after the explosion. If she had gone over the side and was swimming, she would have heard us and answered." Marlin said sadly.

None of those on *Marlinspike* said anything else during the rest of the ride back to *Mallard Cove*. Everyone was trying to process what had happened and cope with the pain of their loss.

BILL AND BETTY awoke when several sheriff's and FBI cars pulled into the marina with their blue lights flashing, racing out to the wharf at the end of the commercial basin. Bill walked to the far end of the dock past the ways only to find crime scene tape blocking it off along with some tight-lipped deputies. He could see several people in jumpsuits with "FBI FORENSIC" lettered on their backs, swarming over a sedan that was lit up by portable floodlights. When he realized there was no getting any details out of the deputies, he headed back toward the *Golden Dolphin.* That's when he noticed Shaker's Gold Line was missing. He stood staring at the empty slip wondering where he would have gone so long after midnight when he saw a boat coming back through the breakwater. As the boat approached, he saw it was *Marlinspike,* and Murph was sitting up front with Casey, who had a hand on his shoulder. Everyone in the boat had on very grim faces, and he noticed Lindsay wasn't with them. He passed the lines to Dawn as Shaker backed the boat in. Bill sensed that something bad had happened, and he was uncharacteristically silent. Casey and Dawn helped a zombie-like Murph up onto the dock, and down to the *Irish Luck*. Marlin stepped up on the dock next to Bill.

"What the hell is going on, Shaker?"

Marlin brought him up to speed, and a visibly shaken Bill followed him back to the *Why Knot*'s bar in the salon where he poured them both large glasses of Pilar rum.

"I can't believe it, Shaker, this just can't have happened. Lindsay can't be gone, she's such a sweet kid. What the hell would she have been doing on the *Grisham*? Why would it have been blown up, and who would have done it? And what are the cops doing with that car?"

"I don't know the answers to any of those questions, Bill. I can't even think straight right now, I keep seeing the image of that explosion; it's etched on my brain. Could be the bomber was aboard and accidentally blew himself up, I don't know. Could be she was the target all along, and some psycho was after her. Apparently, the bomber was a kidnapper as well, but what was his connection to the *Grisham*? There are just too many pieces and this puzzle doesn't seem to want to come together."

"Bill? Bill? Are you in there?" Betty was on the dock, looking for her husband.

"Come on aboard." He was dreading what he had to tell her. Like the others, she was shocked.

"Are you sure, Marlin?"

"The only thing I'm sure of is that the *Grisham* is on the bottom, Betty, and that nobody got off her alive. It looked like the Coasties were recovering some bodies as we left, so hopefully, we should know more soon." He left out the part about seeing a partial body.

"Oh, God. She is so sweet. Was so sweet. I just can't believe it. Who would have done this? Why was she on that boat?" Betty was as distraught as Bill. They both had become attached to Lindsay from the first day that she and Murph had tied up at *Mallard Cove*. "Murph must be going through hell right now."

Marlin nodded grimly. "He looked bad when Casey and Dawn took him over to the *Irish Luck*. Understandably bad. He and Lindsay were made for each other, everyone could see that."

"I'm going to go over there and see if there's anything I can do to help. There's no way I can go back to sleep now, so maybe I can do something for him. Poor Murph." A tear was running down her face.

"I don't know what I could say to Murph, so I'm gonna stay over here for now. That is if you are going to be up and want some company, Shaker."

"It's not like I could go back to sleep either, Bill. Of course, you're welcome to sit up with me, I'd like to have the company. I only met Murph yesterday so, I don't think I should go over there."

After Betty left, the two old friends sat and talked, trying to make sense of what had happened. They tried to recall any details that might aid the sheriff with his investigation, but they both drew a blank. After their initial drinks, neither glass was refilled. The amber liquid had done its job by soothing their frayed nerves, but now each of them wanted a clear head to think. And while it was true that Marlin had only met Murph and Lindsay yesterday, after witnessing the horror that just happened, he wanted answers almost as badly as Bill. While he had originally decided not to move over here in case something like this were to happen, all that changed with that song on the ride back to his old marina. Whatever it was about the song that changed his mind, it now fueled his resolve to do what he could to help find some answers.

Marlin and Bill talked until the sun came up, and the marina started coming alive. Marlin made coffee for both of them, then they walked down the dock to talk with their friends. Today should have been an upbeat day after such a successful party, but instead, the dock had a very somber feel. Bill walked over to the *Kembe II* after he spotted Hard Rock and Gaffer showing up. Marlin saw Casey hanging up his phone in *Predator*'s cockpit. He headed over there where he was waved aboard.

"Any news, Casey?"

"Dawn and Betty are taking turns staying with Murph. He just fell asleep, probably the best thing for him right now. The sheriff won't say anything about what the FBI found in that car, or what the motive might be. He did say that the Coasties recovered two bodies and part of a third, but they were so badly burned and mangled that it'll take DNA testing to identify them. They'll raise what's left of the *Grisham* as soon as possible, and divers are going to look for more remains this morning. Our security contractor is running facial recognition on all the videos they took last night. They'll see if they can identify the bomber in the crowd, but that'll only work if he's got a record."

"None of this makes any sense. So many questions, and so few answers right now." Marlin shook his head.

Wall Street came storming down the dock and stopped behind *Predator*.

"Is it true? Ripper told me that someone bombed the *Grisham* and that Lindsay is dead." His tone wasn't one of sadness, as much as one of imposition.

Casey replied, "Lindsay is missing, and is presumed to have been aboard the *Grisham* when it exploded for reasons that aren't clear yet."

"Reasons that aren't clear yet? Are you serious, or just too stupid to see that someone is targeting us, and he barely missed us all last night? First Murph's truck, now this! We're all lucky that he only got Lindsay. Well, I'm not waiting around to let him finish the job on me, I'm taking my boat and getting the hell out of here before I get blown up, too. I'll send somebody for my car after I get settled because I'm never coming back here." With that, he stormed back down the dock toward the commercial basin.

"Is that guy for real? He was part of their afternoon beer bunch, so he knew Lindsay. What an unfeeling jackass! Good riddance!" Casey said.

Shaker's brow furrowed. Wall Street had put into words kind of what he had felt only yesterday before his change of heart. He didn't know how to respond now, so he just nodded.

16

SHOTS FIRED

In the tech department of ESVA Security over in Norfolk, Rikki's team was already working on the five different camera videos in high-speed mode. Unfortunately, there were almost eight hours of video per camera to run through analysis. So, even running at this faster rate with multiple analyzers, it would take over two hours to go through it all. They were able to access the federal criminal database for comparison, courtesy of some of their post-political life, highly connected protectee clients. What didn't help speed things along was that several in the crowd had DUI, "drunk and disorderly" convictions, and one outstanding warrant for a "failure to appear." These kept setting off alerts and slowing their progress. Some of the males in the sportfishing crowd tended to have a high level of testosterone and a small amount of brains when alcohol became involved.

An hour into it they had a hit that looked promising. The subject's name was Samuel Edwards. He had served time for kidnapping and had been released only two years prior. Rikki followed him in the crowd until he disappeared. The time stamp indicated this was about three minutes before someone made the call to the bomb's burner phone. He then showed back up in the crowd two minutes later. She printed out a screenshot of his face and made a copy of his record.

Rikki sent a short clip of the video to her tablet, then headed to her SUV. She left instructions to call her if anything else came up on the videos, but she didn't think it would. Her gut screamed that this was their guy, even though he had no background in explosives. In this information age, there were so many pages about things like this out there on the internet, especially on the dark web. Anyone with half a brain and bad intentions could learn in a short amount of time enough to do what their bomber had accomplished.

SOMETHING about what Wall Street said had been bothering Marlin, though he couldn't quite put his finger on what it was. In reality, the whole one-sided conversation thing bothered him. But he couldn't blame the guy for wanting to get clear of this marina. He kept running it over and over in his mind, but he always came up empty. Marlin decided that it must have been the way Wall Street said it that bothered him. That, or the fact that he felt guilty himself over finding fault with the guy for hightailing it out of here. He might have even considered it again himself if it wasn't for the people last night that he talked into moving here. He couldn't defend himself to them if he left now too.

Marlin walked slowly down the dock past where Wall Street had already pulled out, headed toward the mouth of the Chesapeake. He could still see *Bull Market* far in the distance just clearing Fisherman's Island and turning toward the southwest. He walked past the ways and out to where the crime scene tape was still blocking off the wharf as it fluttered slightly in the light breeze. It kept him from making the turn out toward the breakwater. Marlin had hoped this walk would clear his head but instead, seeing that tape was just painful. It only added more weight to the burden that was already on his shoulders. That's when it hit him that Lindsay must have come this same way on the last walk she would ever take on earth, and he shivered. He reversed direction and walked back toward the charter boat slips, spotting Baloney and Casey talking behind the *Golden Dolphin*. As he came up to them, he suddenly realized what had been bothering him about what Wall Street had said. He interrupted their conversation.

"Bill! Did you say anything to anyone about finding the bomb yesterday?"

"Ah course not, Shaker. Rikki said not ta say anything ta anyone else, that she had this covered. But I don't know why anybody might figure there could be a bomb aboard the *Grisham*, it was too far away from the crowd. By puttin' that bomb on the patio like he did, it was clear he wanted a big bunch ah casualties."

"Exactly! Casey, did you say anything to anyone?"

"No, we wanted it kept quiet. Where are you going with this?"

Marlin swore, "Dammit! I should have caught it right off the bat. Remember what Wall Street said? 'someone is targeting us, and he barely missed us all last night.' Other than us, the security crew, Murph, and Lindsay, everyone else thought the bomber was only after Murph or Lindsay. We were the only ones who knew about the other bomb, where it was placed, and that he wanted to kill a lot of people with it. Wall Street said the bomber was targeting 'us' and that he missed 'all of us.' Why say that unless he knew about the other device? The bomb on the *Grisham* doesn't fit that statement, only the one on the patio does. How the hell could he have found out about it?"

Casey squinted as he thought. "I don't know, Marlin. It could be a coincidence or, he might have just misspoken."

"Casey, didn't you feel like he was way off base when he said the rest of what he did? I mean, I could see him saying something like that later, but not right after he learned that Lindsay was dead. I'm telling you, all of it only makes sense if he knew about the other bomb, and it not detonating. It *has* to be him."

Baloney looked thoughtful, as he put a cigar in his mouth. It moved from one side to the other as he mulled over what had been said. "Tuna, ya know, Shaker just might be onta something."

At that moment Rikki's SUV came racing into the parking area, stopping next to the trio. She jumped out holding a tablet and some papers and stepped down onto the dock.

"I think we may have identified a suspect." She passed the picture to Casey as Bill and Marlin looked on.

Baloney exclaimed, "Wall Street! At least that's what we call him. His real name's Robert Childers."

Rikki shook her head. "His real name is Samuel Edwards, and he has a prior arrest for kidnapping, though they couldn't get a conviction. It involved a human trafficking ring. He dropped off the radar two years ago. And that's not all, my office just sent me this." She held up her tablet, showing a picture of a sedan driving past the party on the boatyard driveway. It was the car that had been abandoned out by the *Grisham*. "Is this the car that was out on the wharf?"

When Casey nodded, she continued. "We zoomed in and got a face from the backseat, it's the teenage girl from the mall shooting. We couldn't get faces off the driver and front passenger, but somehow all of them are tied to the *Grisham*."

"And this Edwards thing is no coincidence. He's the only one left walking around out of all of them. Somehow Lindsay must have figured it out and gone over to the *Grisham* and gotten caught," Casey said sadly.

"You guys have a lead on who killed Lindsay?" Murph had hadn't been able to sleep and wanted off the boat, away from the now painful memories that haunted it. He had caught the last part of the conversation as he walked up with Dawn.

Baloney said, "It was Wall Street, an' his real name is Edwards. He's a kidnapper and a bomber."

Rikki said, "He's a *suspect*. We don't know for sure that he's the bomber."

Baloney was undeterred. "That sonofabitch was arrested for kidnapping, he lied about his name, an' he knew about the patio bomb. Only way he coulda known is if he was the one who put it there. Let's go get him!" He started down the dock.

"Bill, *hold it*! He's gone." Marlin said.

"Whaddaya mean *gone*?"

"I mean, dock box loaded, lines back on the boat, and gone. *Bull*

Market pulled out half an hour ago." Marlin was mad at himself for not figuring it out sooner and stopping him.

Murph was headed back to his boat when Casey headed him off. "Let the sheriff handle this."

Murph shook his head adamantly, "No way. He's already got a half-hour head start, and he'll be long gone by the time they gear up and get after him. I'm going to catch up to him myself." He motioned toward *Irish Luck*.

"You'll never catch him in the Rybo, you're not that much faster than him. Let's take *Predator*, she's almost twice as fast as *Bull Market*." Casey suggested, and Murph replied with a nod.

Dawn said, "Let's go, we're wasting time!" The group loaded aboard as Casey fired up the big twelve-hundred-horsepower MAN diesels, which could push *Predator* up to a top speed of thirty-nine knots. Murph was laser focused now and handled the bow lines. Bill and Marlin took care of the stern and spring lines and they were clear of the slip in seconds.

Rikki was in the cockpit talking on the phone with Sheriff Roberts who told her to "stand down" and he would get the Coast Guard to handle finding Edwards. Fortunately, at that point, Casey pushed the throttles wide open, and Rikki said, "Sorry, Sheriff, I can't hear you over the engines, I'll have to call you back after we catch up with him."

She climbed up to the flying bridge, joining everyone else. Dawn was in the seat next to Casey, double-checking her pistol and making sure she had a round in the chamber and a full magazine. Murph was standing on the other side of Casey, leaning forward as if to urge more speed out of *Predator*. Bill and Marlin were on the bench seat forward of the console, and Rikki joined them there.

Casey headed Southwest; the same direction *Bull Market* had taken when Shaker had last seen her as she disappeared behind Fisherman's Island. Hopefully, Edwards hadn't changed course, doubled back, or headed offshore. Casey was counting on him feeling safe and cocky, thinking he had gotten away clean. So, it was likely that he'd hold his course. Casey turned on his radar, but on this beautiful

Sunday morning, the water was already getting crowded. Here at the mouth of the Chesapeake, there were dozens of potential targets running in southerly directions, any one of which could be the Bertram. Casey stuck to his course.

"Keep lookin', Tuna! As fast as this rig is, we oughta see him soon."

"We will if he kept going this way, Bill. Hopefully, he was heading to Lynnhaven inlet or Thimble Shoal channel." Casey glanced over at Murph, who had a pair of high-power binoculars, checking out every speck on the horizon.

"I've got what I think is the Bertram, it's about the right size, and it's dead ahead. Looks like she's idling, about three miles up, heading for Thimble Shoal. It's got to be *Bull Market*. There are a couple of Coast Guard boats just off the tunnel islands, and there's a Navy Seahawk helicopter overhead there, too." Murph was now completely focused, intent on getting answers and revenge.

Baloney said, "That aircraft carrier *Harry S Truman* is supposed ta head ta sea today. It's flood tide, so she must be coming out. The Coasties are there ta keep sightseers away. There's a Naval Vessel Protection Zone in place around her. That means all vessels within 500 yards have ta be at idle, and they'll fire any boat within a hundred yards. They've got Sea Whiz systems onboard, and they won't hesitate to use 'em after what happened with the USS Cole."

"What's a Sea Whiz?" Dawn asked Bill.

"It's slang for Close-In *Weapons Systems* or, *CWIS*. The biggest one aboard is the Phalanx 20-millimeter Gatling gun. 4,500 rounds per minute. You don't wanna get anywhere near her, 'specially when she's the most vulnerable right there between the tunnel islands. Nobody else is allowed in that channel at the same time as her when she passes through. That's when her crew is likely ta be the most nervous an' trigger happy, an' they can turn a boat this size into Swiss cheese in the blink of an eye. Edwards must just be taking his time until the Truman clears the channel before he cranks up and heads over inta the bay."

The CBBT had four channels that taller flybridge-equipped boats like *Bull Market* could use, and Thimble Shoals was the last one to the south. It was Edwards's bad luck because if he had changed course and used any of the first three, he would have already gotten into the bay. They wouldn't have a clue which direction he had headed, and chances are they wouldn't have spotted him. They were just lucky that Marlin had gotten a bead on Edwards's heading when he left.

Casey kept his throttles wide open as he closed the gap between *Predator* and *Bull Market*, now about a half mile apart, and two miles away from the channel. Wall Street must have recognized Casey's boat and figured it wasn't a good thing that he was there and running straight for him. *Bull Market* jumped up on a plane as he tried to get away, but *Predator* had the speed to close the gap between them. They were about a mile from the channel when Casey pulled out from behind the Bertram and crossed her wake as he moved to pull alongside. *Bull Market* turned, its wake catching the side of *Predator*'s bow, making her heel over slightly, and then Edwards turned, trying to sideswipe her. Casey dodged him, backed off the throttles, and matched his speed as he spotted Edwards on the bridge of his main deck. He raised a pistol and began firing at them.

Casey yelled, "Gun! Everybody down!"

Everyone on the flybridge ducked except for Murph. The low windscreen next to him shattered as Edwards's bullet found the plexiglass. Without even flinching Murph fired several rounds back at Edwards who then ducked behind his bench seat. Then he ran through the hatch and down the steps into the cabin. When he came back up into view a few seconds later, he was holding a gun to the head of the girl from the mall. Both of them were now on deck, facing toward *Predator*. Even though she was half a foot shorter than he was, Edwards had her in front of him, using her as a shield. Her arms were out in front, and they could see she was bound at her wrists with duct tape. Edwards used his left hand to reach over and behind him to turn the wheel. He steered *Bull Market* out toward the ocean, away from the channel and the Coast Guard boats. Casey matched his turn, then pulled back across his wake and behind the Bertram, now only twenty yards directly astern. They saw Edwards grab a microphone as the VHF radio crackled.

"Shaw, shut down or I shoot the girl." He was broadcasting on Channel 16, which was monitored by most boats. It was also the marine distress channel.

"Vessel on Channel 16 identify yourself. This is the United States Coast Guard, Portsmouth."

Ignoring the Coast Guard he continued, "You heard me, Shaw, shut down or the girl dies."

Casey picked up his microphone. "Coast Guard, this is the fishing vessel *Predator.* There is a hostage situation aboard the yacht *Bull Market*, please stand by. Edwards, nobody else needs to get hurt, so put the gun down."

"*Predator*, Coast Guard Portsmouth. What is your location?"

Casey didn't answer and kept focused ahead. He saw what might be an opportunity coming up. "Murph, get ready."

"I see it, Case."

Edwards was still facing aft and was both distracted and worried by Casey knowing his real name. He didn't see the huge wake from a passing boat approaching his port quarter, though Casey and Murph both did. Casey had owned a Bertram that he and Murph fished on for many years. They knew this wake was coming at the absolute worst, most bone-jarring angle for *Bull Market*'s deep vee hull. Edwards must have felt the initial rise over the first wave because he turned to his right. Then the bow dropped and rose before dropping again, slamming into the face of the next, much steeper wave in the set and throwing both he and the girl off balance. He took the gun away from the girl's head as he reached for a handhold. She saw her opportunity and dove to the deck in front of him. Unfortunately, she caught her head on the corner of the bench seat and then fell on her side, totally limp.

This was the break Murph had been waiting for. He adjusted his aim for the movement of the Bertram and the wake, he got off half a dozen rounds before *Predator* hit the same set of waves and it forced him to brace himself. But several of his bullets had found their mark.

Edwards fell over backward through the hatch and down the companionway steps. He didn't reappear.

Now *Bull Market* was headed out to sea with her engines at full throttle, and no one at the controls. The hydraulic steering was keeping the rudders locked and the boat pointed straight. The Bertram would hold her heading and track straight so long as she wasn't tossed around by any other large wakes.

"Case, we've got to get on board and stop her. That kid hasn't moved and must be hurt." Murph said, seemingly unfazed by what had just occurred.

"What do you have in mind?"

"Your bow is high enough and has enough flare so that if you get in close enough, I can jump onboard." Murph sounded confident.

"Are you *nuts*?" Baloney was just picking himself up off the deck. "That friggin' rooster tail is three feet high, an' the turbulence will throw the bow all over the place. You miss and hit the water you'll be back through our props and chopped inta pieces. Tell me you were kiddin'."

The rooster tail occurs in the most turbulent part of a boat's wake and starts right behind the stern. It happens when the displaced water from each side of the hull recombines into a curved and narrow hump of water. Depending on the boat's speed, hull design and displacement, it can be really long and high, as it was behing the Bertram.

Murph looked Baloney straight in the eye. "We've got to stop that boat before it runs somebody over. That girl now is the only one left who holds the key to figuring out what this was all about, and why Lindsay was murdered. I have to know, Bill."

Baloney grabbed both of Murph's shoulders, "Murph, let the Coast Guard handle this. They can drop someone onboard from a helicopter."

Dawn spoke up. "We don't have enough time. Look where she is heading!" She was pointing beyond the Bertram. Just under a mile, dead ahead, a huge freighter lay at anchor, waiting for a slot to open at the harbor in Norfolk. It was lying broadside to *Bull Market*, directly in her path.

Casey said, “We have less than two minutes if we’re going to pull this off.”

Baloney looked at Casey, “If you’re serious about this, I’ll have ta direct ya from the bow, to let ya know how close ya are.”

Casey nodded. “Get going.”

“I’m coming too. You can’t go over there alone. He’s armed, we aren’t sure he’s dead, and you’ll need cover.” Rikki said as she turned and climbed down the ladder, leaving no room for discussion, quickly followed by Murph and Baloney. Shaker and Dawn stayed on the flybridge with Casey.

Baloney, Rikki, and Murph appeared up on the bow just as Casey started closing the gap between them and the Bertram. The isinglass curtains were rolled up on her elevated aft deck, so they would have a clean jump over the railing and onto the deck.

Predator’s bow was pitched way up at an angle, running at what was for her a slow cruise. Bill put one foot against the two-inch high varnished toe rail which ran around the edge of the bow. It was there to help prevent anyone from going over the side. He looked down at the narrowing gap, motioning Casey forward with one hand. As they closed the gap and the bow got into the turbulence of the rooster tail, *Predator* got a little squirrely. Her bow was now making jerky motions from side to side. Baloney was still braced against the toe rail with that foot and was somehow able to maintain his balance without pitching over the side himself. He held his arms apart as they closed the gap, then moved his hands in closer, representing the distance left, as Casey delicately worked the throttles. Finally, Baloney clasped both hands together, just as Murph and Rikki leaped over the Bertram’s railing onto the covered aft deck, their pistols up and ready.

Casey quickly backed off the throttles as Baloney retreated to the center of the bow’s deck. Casey crossed over the Bertram’s starboard wake again, pulling alongside as Murph took the controls and turned the Bertram hard to port, with Casey following suit a mere three hundred yards away from the freighter.

With Murph now at the wheel, Rikki had gone to the aid of the girl while also keeping her pistol trained on the cabin door. It turned out the girl had only been knocked out when she hit her head on the corner of the seat. She had a big knot on her forehead but was already coming around. Rikki gave a "thumbs up' in *Predator*'s direction. Murph then slowed the Bertram to idle speed and shifted both gears into neutral. He heard Casey on the radio contacting the Coast Guard again and he was directed to switch over from the hailing channel to a less busy one. He was just about to follow along when suddenly two muffled shots rang out from below, and he felt a hot poker shoved into his right thigh. His leg crumpled and he fell to the deck.

Over on *Predator's* bridge, Bill had just rejoined them when they heard the shots and saw Murph drop.

"Coast Guard, shots fired. Two of my crew have boarded *Bull Market*, and one is now down. We need help out here!"

The four could do nothing but watch as they saw Rikki go through the hatch and down the steps into the cabin. After what seemed like hours but was only seconds, three more muffled shots rang out.

"Case, get us over there! Me an' Shaker are gonna go help Murph an' Rikki." Baloney said. Casey nodded and passed him his pistol since Baloney was unarmed. Then the two made their way up to the bow and climbed onto the now drifting Bertram as soon as Casey pulled alongside the aft deck.

Baloney headed straight to Murph and put pressure on his leg wound while Shaker went below into the cabin. Casey updated the Coast Guard over the radio while he and Dawn stood by on the flybridge.

RIKKI HAD BEEN bent over checking on the girl when she heard the shots and saw fiberglass shards flying up from the deck. She knew racing over to Murph might get her shot as well; she needed to concentrate on neutralizing the threat. The master stateroom would be right under this raised deck. Either Edwards had survived and made it that far, or he had an accomplice aboard who knew the boat well enough to know where to shoot through the deck to hit someone at the helm. She carefully passed through the hatch and down the steps, noting a pool of blood at the bottom. She saw bloody smears heading back through the open master stateroom door where Edwards either dragged himself or had been dragged by an accomplice. Rikki looked in and saw that Edwards was propped against the base of an "L"-shaped couch, talking to someone beyond her sightline. He spotted her, swung his pistol, and fired, his shot going wide. Rikki's two shots were good, the first to his mid-chest, and the second to the center of his forehead, finishing him.

Slowly and carefully Rikki passed through the doorway, drawing down on the other person in the room. She wasn't prepared for what she found.

17

HELL TO PAY

Shaker crept cautiously down the steps into the cabin and saw the blood trail. Carefully he peered into the stateroom he spotted Edwards's lifeless form on the floor. He looked left and got the shock of his life.

Rikki looked at him and said, “I've got this. Check the rest of the boat for any others. And watch your ass.” He did as she directed but found no one else, and he returned to the aft stateroom to help. The three made their way up and out of the cabin and moved over to where Baloney was attending to a moaning Murph. He was lying on the deck with his eyes clenched shut in pain, his left thigh, and the seat of his pants soaked in blood.

“Babe, you're hurt!”

Murph raised his head and opened his eyes, looked over, and saw the last person on earth he ever expected to. “Lindsay? You're alive! How? We thought you died on the *Grisham*.” He saw that Rikki and Shaker were having to help steady her. “You're hurt too?”

With their help, she sat on the deck next to him as he put his head back down and closed his eyes and winced. “I was never on the *Grisham*, and why would you think I died? I'm fine, but Wall Street used duct tape on my wrists and legs. It was too tight, and I'm only now getting some feeling back in them."

Baloney said, "Ya don't know how glad I am to see ya, Lindsay! Looks like this is a through and through gunshot wound. Went in his thigh, and out through the left butt cheek. I'll keep puttin' pressure on the thigh, but his butt is all yours." He winked at her. "He's gonna be fine. See if you can get him to stop moaning though. He's goin' for an Oscar."

Lindsay put pressure on his higher wound. It might be that he was more worried about her, or perhaps it was a touch of machismo, but Murph did stop moaning. He looked over at her and managed a wan smile. "I thought you were gone."

She returned the smile, "Why? I was wondering what was taking you so damned long to come and find me."

"We followed your phone; it was on the *Grisham* when it took off and blew up."

"Wait, the *Grisham* blew up?"

Baloney answered, "They all took off after it 'cause your phone tracker thing said ya were onboard, but it exploded before they caught up with it. Nobody got off alive so, we all thought ya were dead. Shaker over there finally figured it all out, an' Rikki showed up after she checked the videos an' saw Wall Street disappear when he tried ta blow up the party. Said his real name is Edwards."

Shaker chimed in from over where he was tending to the girl who was now sitting up. "You mean it *was* Edwards. Murph winged him, but Rikki finished the job."

Lindsay nodded. "Wall Street, or Edwards, took my phone after he tasered me. I got knocked out when I fell and hit my head on the dock. He carried me into that stateroom and wrapped me up in duct tape just as I was coming to. I just figured my phone was gone because he didn't want me calling for help. I thought you guys would search all the boats, and I'd be able to knock my head against the hull or do something, so then you'd hear me. But a few hours later he cranked up and we started running, so I figured I was a goner. He said he was going to sell me because I'd bring a great price." She shuddered. "I always felt like he was creepy, but I had no idea he was a total psycho."

Shaker replied, "We would have searched all the boats, but then he tossed us that red herring, making us follow the *Grisham,* which tricked us into thinking you died. He came over ranting and raving about us all nearly getting blown up last night and said he was leaving because of it. Talk about an Oscar-worthy performance! If he hadn't slipped up by talking about a bomb that he shouldn't have known about, and if Rikki hadn't found what she did, we might never have found you."

"But you had already seen through it, what I found just clinched it," Rikki said. "And, if he had left five minutes earlier, he might have made it through Thimble Shoals channel, and we would have been stuck on this side waiting on that carrier while he got away." Just then her phone rang. Casey and Dawn had seen Lindsay and wanted an update.

Lindsay was confused. "Stuck how?"

Baloney pointed to the west. "By that."

The *Harry S. Truman* was now clear of the channel, about two miles away, and headed out to sea to join her escort ships. Even at this distance, the size of the huge ship was impressive. Two of the eighty-seven-foot Coast Guard patrol boats that had been guarding her through Thimble Shoals were now half a mile away and closing on their position.

"Casey, that's Lindsay, she's alive!" it overjoyed Dawn to see her friend.

Casey called Rikki, who told him Edwards was dead, and that both Lindsay and the girl from the mall would be fine. But she said they needed to get Murph to a hospital though his wounds didn't appear to be life-threatening. Then she had to hang up because Sheriff Roberts was calling.

"Rik said Lindsay is okay. Edwards is dead, and Murph's wounded, but not seriously. The girl's okay, too."

Dawn had tears running down her cheeks. "I can't believe she's alive. She must have been aboard *Bull Market* all along. That bastard Edwards had us all fooled, and I'm glad he's dead. No trial, no chance for acquittal or parole, just dead."

COAST GUARDSMEN from both patrol boats boarded *Predator* and *Bull Market* fully armed and in tactical gear, confiscating all their weapons. A medic used clot patches on Murph's wounds, and they put him on a stretcher. They transferred him across to one of the patrol boats, along with Lindsay and the girl. All three would go to the hospital, the latter with a female FBI agent assigned to ride and stay with her when they reached the shore. After getting initial statements from everyone else aboard, they instructed Casey and Baloney to follow the lead patrol boat for the ride into Portsmouth under the watchful eyes of several armed Coast Guardsmen. Baloney would run *Bull Market*, with the second patrol boat bringing up the rear. As they turned toward Hampton Roads and the Elizabeth River after clearing Thimble Shoals, they saw numerous cars with blue lights racing toward the Virginia Beach end of the bridge. They would have quite a group waiting for them when they tied up. On seeing this, Rikki made a quick call on her phone.

They directed both boats to a small dock at the huge Coast Guard complex at Craney Island Creek off the Elizabeth River. Besides numerous patrol boats, this was also home to several buoy tenders, a buoy maintenance center, a training center, and the USCG center, training center, and the USCG Command Engineering Center. Altogether, two dozen ships, boats, and their crews all called this base home.

As Rikki had expected, there was a large group of people waiting for them to tie up including members of the FBI ACTeam plus Sheriff Roberts and a few of his deputies. They all looked unhappy, and Roberts looked almost irate. He was one of the first aboard *Bull Market* after she tied up, and even before Murph, Lindsay, and the girl were taken to a waiting ambulance.

"What the hell part of 'stand down' don't you understand?" He was addressing Rikki. He turned to one of his deputies, "Take her into custody. For now, we'll charge her with obstruction of justice. That may get upgraded to a murder charge after we finish our investigation into the shooting." The deputy put Rikki in handcuffs.

One of the FBI agents hung up his phone and pulled the sheriff aside. What he told him didn't help the sheriff's attitude, as he exploded. "What do you mean my department is off this case? We were conducting a joint investigation!"

The agent said, "This is from way above my pay grade, Sheriff. It would be a good idea to take those handcuffs off Ms. Jenkins, too."

Sheriff Roberts glared at the agent then at Rikki and nodded to his deputy, who released her. Then he and his deputies stepped onto the dock and quickly left. The FBI agent came over to Rikki.

"You've got friends in some pretty high places."

She shrugged and smiled. "My company does work for interesting people sometimes."

"Still, I'd be careful not to do one mile per hour over the speed limit in his county. He doesn't look like the type to let a grudge go," the agent said.

"Thanks for the good advice. Yeah, I bet he was all set to hold a press conference to claim credit for taking down Edwards. I don't think I'll be getting a card from him this year at Christmas." She chuckled.

A tall man in a Coast Guard uniform loaded with stripes and ribbons smiled as he approached. "Hello, neighbor. Stirring up trouble again are you?" ESVA Security's Norfolk complex housed not just their tech department, but also their marine assets. It was just upriver from the Coast Guard base, and she had known the base commander for some time. Her group had come up on the Coast Guard radar because of their go-fast boats that all but screamed "drug smugglers." A phone call had straightened that out and created an opportunity for face-to-face introductions.

"Hello, Captain. I'm just trying to prevent more trouble. This guy Edwards was behind a string of bombings on ESVA, as well as several kidnappings along the east coast. The world is a much better place these days without him breathing."

He nodded. "I received a call from Atlantic Coast Command about this. They got a call from Washington, but if I had to guess, I'd say you already knew that. So, we'll make our part short and sweet. I'm sure you will want to check on your friends over at the hospital, but we'll need more detailed statements from each of you first. Then we'll have someone drive you over there. Good to see you again, Ms. Jenkins, I'm glad you came out on the winning side of this one." He shook her hand and left.

THE SHOOTING PART of the investigation was a joint one between the FBI and the Coast Guard because it had happened in US territorial waters and not on shore. The FBI sat in as a courtesy because of their investigation into Edwards. As the base commander had promised, after an hour of questioning in a building on the base they were finished and transported over to the hospital.

Murph's wound was confirmed as a "through and through" limited to muscle and not hitting any bone or major arteries. He had several stitches and several painful days ahead. But he would only be in the hospital for a couple of days as they watched out for any infection to set in. They had removed several fragments of fiberglass from the wound that had come from the deck. The surface Gelcoat could harbor some nasty germs, and they were administering a strong antibiotic intravenously as a precaution.

Neither Lindsay nor the girl had any lingering effects from their head injuries other than lumps and bruises. However, the girl's trauma wasn't limited to a knock on her skull. The real damage was from being held captive by the sadistic kidnapper and rapist, Kamal. Those psychological wounds were deep, and she would need a lot of help before they could begin to heal. But reuniting her with her family would be a good start, and she would leave soon along with the agent they assigned to her, heading back to New Jersey. During questioning, she provided details about the container setup, how many girls had been shipped out, and when they had left. These details had provided enough clues to identify which ship they had loaded the container aboard. Several Navy ships were being dispatched to intercept that freighter and rescue those onboard.

Lindsay wanted to stay at the hospital with Murph, but he insisted that she go back to *Mallard Cove* along with everyone else. She hadn't slept in two days and needed a good night's sleep in their bed. They had given him pain medication that had him nodding off anyway, so she didn't put up much of a fight. They went back to the Coast Guard base and loaded aboard *Predator* for the hour-long ride back.

Shaker and Baloney were leaning against the aft railing on the flybridge. As they idled down the river past Naval Base Norfolk, Baloney lit up his noxious cigar as Shaker pretended to gag.

"I thought you only gassed people on your own boat!"

"Nope. I light one up every time I'm out on the water, unless Betty's aboard, she doesn't like 'em. It's my good luck thing, and with all the commotion I forgot ta light up this morning, so we're lucky ta still be alive. Hey, Shaker, now that you're over at *Mallard Cove* with us, maybe we can fish together sometime on a day off. I'll even get you your own cigar." Baloney was grinning from ear to ear, making it hard for Shaker to decide if he was serious or not about the stogie. He hoped Baloney was only kidding about that part.

Dawn and Lindsay were sitting on the bench in front of the flybridge helm. Dawn said, "Bill might have a great idea there. Maybe we should go fishing together. It's bound to be less stressful than our last shopping trip, but we would ban Bill's cigars. What do you think, Linds?" Looking over at Lindsay, Dawn realized that she had fallen asleep. She smiled at her friend and then settled back against the seat.

THEY PULLED into *Mallard Cove* and Casey saw that the *Golden Dolphin* was missing. Casey looked startled and turned toward Baloney, who had a curious look. "What? I had a half-day charter today, remember?

Couldn't let 'em down, so I called B2 ta run the boat while I was gone. The kid needs that kinda responsibility now and then since he got his captain's license last month. A friend ah his is mating for him today. If things get as busy next year as I think they will, I might get another boat for him ta run for me.

"Ya know, Tuna, there are only a few reasons I'd miss a charter. One of the biggest is having my friends' backs. Murph and Lindsay are worth it. You are too, but don't go gettin' in trouble just ta test it." He grinned then the grin became an even wider smile.

"Uh, oh. I'm beginning to be able to read you, Bill, and you're scaring me already."

"Well, I was just thinkin', Tuna. Ya know, all my beer is out on the water aboard my boat."

"Help yourself to mine… Baloney."

"Don't mind if I do! Hey, Shaker, let's get this rig tied up, and then the beer's on me!"

They both headed down the bridge ladder as Casey backed *Predator* into her slip. Dawn came around to Casey. "I thought we were headed back to *Bayside* today."

"Nope. We can't leave now; we still have beer left aboard that Baloney hasn't given away yet." He cocked his head and said, "You know, things like this remind you how short life can be. There's nothing at the office that can't wait another day or two. Let's help get Murph home, then we can take our time and troll back to the *Bluffs* along the beach. See if we can't run into those mackerel."

She put her arms around his neck and looked into his eyes. "I like the way you think. But only if you make some of your famous smoked fish dip out of them."

"Deal."

~

Monday morning…

Baloney looked sadly at the shell that had been the patio and the dining room. The construction crew wasn't wasting any time stripping the interior, eager to get to the rebuilding phase. "I feel like they just evicted me."

Kari Albury came up behind him. "Not evicted, only moved temporarily. You didn't notice that all the chairs and tables are now under the tent over there?" She pointed to the temporary home of the Beer-Thirty-Bunch in the parking area behind his slip.

"Nah, I missed that, I was staring at what was goin' on over here. Ya don't waste any time, do ya?"

She beamed. "I try not to. How is Murph? We all heard about what happened."

"He'll live. Probably get a lot of mileage out of the whole thing, too. But what you did gives me an idea." He told her what he had in mind.

EPILOGUE

Two days later, Lindsay pulled up with Murph in her car. The whole group was lined up in front of the tent, blocking the view. Casey came over and helped Lindsay get him out of the car and on his feet and crutches as everyone moved aside, revealing a plush lounge chair with a super soft pad and a huge pillow. A small cooler flanked it on one side, and a low table was on the other, with a pair of binoculars sitting on top.

Lindsay said, “This was Baloney’s idea. Since you are supposed to take it easy for a few more days, he figured you could see almost everything from here.”

“Yeah, Murph, just don’t get used to it long-term!” Baloney roared.

“Somehow, I don’t think you would let me.”

“Darned right I wouldn’t. Oh, hey, one more get-well gift. These always bring me luck.” Baloney handed him a cigar.

Ripper said, “Yeah, but they almost kill all the rest of us!” The group laughed.

“You guys just don’t appreciate a good half-dollar cigar!” Baloney frowned.

Spud said, “We would, but there ain’t no such thing!” More laughter.

Casey and Baloney each took an arm and helped lower Murph into his lounger as the rest of the Beer-Thirty-Bunch settled into their relocated chairs.

Murph looked pleased to be back. "Case, I thought you would be back at *Bayside* by now?"

"What, and not be here for the unveiling of your new throne? No way I'd have missed this. Dawn and I are heading back in the morning. But we'll be down often to check in on you."

"It'll be good to have you guys around." He paused a minute. "You know, a few things are bothering me about what happened. Edwards was a psycho, but he was smart and had all of us fooled for quite a while. Why would he blow up his own boat?"

Dawn answered. "Rikki talked to the FBI. They got enough info off his computer and from the girl to figure out most of it. He was the brains behind a human trafficking ring. He wanted this property for it because it fit the *Grisham's* requirements so well. But like Cetta, he didn't know it was going to come on the market until after you two had already tied it up. And he was stretched thin after moving from New Jersey, so he needed to get it as cheaply as he could. Killing off the competition was his way of achieving that."

"Then why blow up the *Grisham*?"

"He always had an alternate plan. The Turks were becoming a liability, taking bigger risks and creating too much exposure. When they bailed out of the farmhouse and barely got away, he probably figured things would go south fast, and he needed to throw the police off his trail. The girl said he flew into a rage after he found her on the *Grisham*; the Turk's leader had been ordered to kill her days before. He was taking her off the *Grisham* and over to his boat when they ran into Lindsay who recognized her.

"The *Grisham* was getting close to the end of her lifespan, anyway. The alternate plan was to blow up the *Grisham* with the three Turks aboard, making it look like an accident or sabotage. They would cover this under his insurance policy and would be made payable to his shell corporation, so he wouldn't look in any way connected to it. Now he was screwed because Lindsay and the girl could link him to it. So, he couldn't leave them around to talk about it. Putting her phone onboard was an afterthought. But he knew once it was traced, this would stop people from trying to find her. He only needed one body to be identified to have it all circle around back to the mall shooter and the blame would stay with the dead Turks."

Murph was processing what Dawn said, but there were still gaps. "So, he was getting out of human trafficking?"

Dawn shook her head. "Just re-staffing, re-tooling, and moving again since his bomb failed and he couldn't get *Mallard Cove*. He had been following an online auction for a barge with a crane and a tugboat as a backup plan. Barges are stable, and they draw a lot less water than the *Grisham*. It's not unusual to see one running around with a container and crane aboard. He had also pulled up a listing for a piece of wooded property between here and the *Bluffs*. It had an access road and a wide canal running well back into it. Plenty of privacy, and an easy purchase. Plus he wouldn't need the farm anymore because they would be able to stage everything on the barge with no prying eyes around. Something he didn't have here."

"One smart psychopath."

Dawn nodded. "Makes an even better dead psychopath."

Lindsay pulled up a chair next to Murph. "I've been thinking."

Murph answered, "Uh, oh."

"No, now hear me out. We will be here either eight or nine months a year, right?"

"Yes?"

"I love living here in the marina, but sometimes it's nice to get off the boat, too."

He said, "I agree with you so far..."

"Well, hearing about that barge got me thinking. What if we put one of those house barges in here? They're more like a house than the Rybo, but there's still no grass to cut." She beamed and looked hopefully at Murph.

He looked at her, then across the basin. "Why not? We can put it over there on the private side and have *Irish Luck* in the slip next to it. Maybe get a big one with a loft bedroom and a sundeck."

She sighed, reached over, and took his hand. "You're serious? I thought I'd have to do a lot more to sell the idea. I love you, babe!"

"Backatcha. Figured I knew how much until I thought you were gone forever."

"Me, too. But as corny as it sounds, I figured you would come find and rescue me."

"I get Rikki and Marlin to do all my light work."

She squeezed his hand. "And it's a good thing you did since you fell down on the job."

"Not happening again, I promise."

Murph lay back and looked at Lindsay and their marina. He realized there were a few things in life worth fighting for, and two of them were the ones you love and your home. He had just fought for both of those and won. His life with Lindsay had turned out to be an exciting adventure so far, but now he figured things should start to calm down around them. As he looked around at his group of new and old friends, he realized it might not. But it sure promised to be interesting...

THE ADVENTURES of the *Mallard Cove* gang continue in Coastal Adventure Book #2, Coastal Cousins.

GLOSSARY

I grew up on the water in South Florida, and I have an extensive boating background. I've worked on boats, built them, re-built them, and spent a good amount of time in boatyards. I've always loved boats, and ever since I was a pre-teenager, I haven't gone longer than six months without owning at least one. Most of my friends are boaters, too. So it's easy for me to forget that not everyone is as familiar with the jargon as my friends and me, which is something that I've now been reminded of on more than one occasion. (My apologies to those readers that I ended up sending to the dictionary!) To make amends, here's a (growing) list of uniquely nautical terms and words that have been included in several of my books. Bear in mind that these definitions are based on my own usage and experience. Things can be different from one region to another. For instance, you can fish for stripers in Montauk, New York, but here in Virginia, we fish for rockfish. But the true name for the target species is "striped bass."

So, here are the definitions of some of the more confusing words, at least as I know them. We'll start with a half dozen simple ones, then move on to those that are more complex:

- **Bow:** the front of the boat.
- **Stern:** back of the boat.
- **Port:** the left side of the boat.
- **Starboard:** the right side of the boat.
- **Aft:** the rear of the boat.
- **Forward:** (fore) the front of the boat.
- **Bow Thruster:** a propeller in a tube that is mounted from side to side through the bow below the waterline, allowing the captain more maneuverability and control when docking especially in adverse winds and currents. Powered by an electric or hydraulic motor.
- **Bulkhead:** boat wall.
- **Center Console:** a type of boat with a raised helm console in the middle of the boat with space on each side to walk around. Most also incorporate a built-in bench seat or cooler seat in the front.
- **Chine:** The longitudinal area running fore and aft where the bottom meets the side. It can be rounded or "sharp." They hurt when the boat rocks and it meets your head when you are swimming next to it. Trust me on that.
- **Circle Hook:** a fishhook designed to get caught in the corner of a fish's mouth. Greatly reduces the mortality of fish that are released or that break the line.
- **Citation:** at an airport, it's a type of jet made by Cessna. But here in Virginia, it's a slip of paper suitable for framing, issued by the state confirming that you caught a fish that's considered large for its particular species. Or it can be a speeding ticket, either on water or land. I like the fish kind better.
- **Covering Board:** a flat surface at the top of a gunwale usually made out of teak or fiberglass, that's used as a step for boarding and for mounting recessed rod holders.
- **Deck:** what floors on boats are called.

- **Fighting Chair:** a specialized chair that can be turned to face a fish. Mounted on a sturdy stanchion with a built-in gimbal, the chair allows the angler to use the attached footrest to use their legs and body to gain more leverage on a large fish. Most of today's fighting chairs are based on the design by my late friend John Rybovich.
- **Fish Box:** a built-in storage box for the day's catch. They can be either elevated in the stern, or in the deck with a flush-mounted lid. Some of the higher-end sportfish boats have cooling systems or automatic ice makers that continually add ice throughout the trip.
- **Fishing Cockpit:** the lower aft deck on a sport fisherman that usually contains a fighting chair, fish box, baitwell, and tackle center. Surrounded on three sides by the gunwales and the stern. The cockpit deck is usually just above the waterline, with scuppers that drain overboard. Can get flooded when backing down hard on a big fish.
- **Flying Bridge (Flybridge):** a permanently mounted helm area on top of the wheelhouse. Can be open or enclosed.
- **Following Sea:** when the waves are moving toward the boat from behind the stern.
- **Gaff:** a large, usually barbless hook at the end of a pole, used for landing fish. They come in different sizes and lengths.
- **Gangway (Gangplank):** a removable ramp or set of stairs attached to the side of larger boats to allow easier access for boarding from a dock. Usually hinged to allow for tide variation.
- **Gear:** marine transmission which has forward, neutral, and reverse.
- **Gimbal:** there are a few types, but the ones in my books are rod holders with swivels built into fighting chairs.
- **Gin Pole:** a vertical pole next to the gunwale usually rigged with a block and tackle and used for hauling large

fish aboard. These used to be quite common until John Rybovich invented the transom door fifty years ago.

- **Gunwale (pronounced gun-nul):** aft side area of a boat above the waterline, also the area on either side of a fishing cockpit.
- **Hatch:** a hole in a deck or bulkhead with a cover that may be hinged or completely removable. On a sport fisherman, the door into the wheelhouse may be called either a hatch or a door.
- **Head:** a bathroom, or a marine toilet.
- **Helm:** the area that includes the steering and engine controls. In many sportfishing boats, the controls are mounted on a helm pod, a wood box with radiused edges that juts out of a cabinet or bulkhead.
- **Keys Conch:** a person born in the Florida Keys. You can be born in Miami and move to the Keys an hour later, then live down there the rest of your life, and you will still NEVER be a Conch. They are usually very tough and independent characters.
- **Lean Seat:** a high bench seat usually found behind the helm of a center console. Designed to be leaned against or sat upon. May have storage built-in under the seat section.
- **Mezzanine Deck:** a shallow, raised deck on a sportfish just forward of the fishing cockpit, and aft of the wheelhouse bulkhead. Usually contains aft-facing bench seating for anglers to comfortably watch the baits that are being trolled behind the boat.
- **Outriggers:** long aluminum poles on sportfishing boats that are raked up and aft from up alongside the wheelhouse. They are extended outward when fishing, having clips on lines that carry the fishing lines out away from the boat, creating a wider spread.
- **Pilot Boat:** a smaller boat designed to handle all kinds of seas, whose sole purpose is delivering and retrieving a

captain with extensive local knowledge to larger boats approaching or leaving a port.

- **Rod Holder:** As the name suggests, a device that a fishing rod butt is inserted into to hold it steady. There are recessed types that are mounted in covering boards, and exposed ones attached to railings or tower legs.
- **Salon:** a living room area of a boat's cabin.
- **Scuppers:** deck or cockpit drains.
- **SeaKeeper Gyro:** a stabilizing gyro that almost eliminates roll in boats.
- **Shaft:** attaches a propeller to the gear.
- **Sheer Line:** the rail edge where the foredeck meets the side of the hull.
- **Sonar/Fish Finder:** electronic underwater 'radar' that displays the sea floor, and anything between it and the boat.
- **Sportfisherman (Sportfish):** a unique style of boat designed specifically for fishing.
- **Spread:** the arrangement of the baits being towed while trolling.
- **Stem:** the forwardmost edge of the bow.
- **Stern:** the farthest aft part of the boat, also called the transom.
- **Tackle Center:** a cabinet in the fishing cockpit or the center console which holds hooks, swivels, leads, and other fishing supplies.
- **(Tuna) Tower:** an aluminum pipe structure located above the house or the flybridge designed to hold spotters or riders, and may or may not have an additional helm.
- **Transom:** stern.
- **Transom (Tuna) Door:** a door in the stern just above the waterline, designed for boating large fish, but also useful for retrieving swimmers and divers.
- **Trough:** the lowest point between waves.

- **Wheel (Propeller):** slang for a prop.
- **Wheel (Steering):** controls the boat's direction.
- **Wheelhouse (House):** the cabin section of a boat which sometimes contains an enclosed helm.

ABOUT THE AUTHOR

Don Rich is the author of the bestselling Coastal Adventure Series. Don's books are set mainly in the mid-Atlantic because of his love for this stretch of coastline. A fifth-generation Florida native who grew up on the water, he has spent a good portion of his life on, in, under, or beside it.

He now makes his home in central Virginia. When he's not writing or watching another fantastic mid-Atlantic sunset, he can often be found on the Chesapeake or the Atlantic with a fishing rod in his hand.

Don loves to hear from readers, and you can reach him via email at contact@donrichbooks.com

ALSO BY DON RICH

(Check my website www.DonRichBooks.com for the current list of all my book titles.

The Coastal Beginnings Series:

(The prelude to the Coastal Adventure Series)

- COASTAL CHANGES
- COASTAL TREASURE
- COASTAL RULES
- COASTAL BLUFFS

The Coastal Adventure Series:

- COASTAL CONSPIRACY
- COASTAL COUSINS
- COASTAL PAYBACKS
- COASTAL TUNA
- COASTAL CATS
- COASTAL CAPER
- COASTAL CULPRIT
- COASTAL CURSE
- COASTAL JURY
- COASTAL CURRENCY
- COASTAL CRUISE

Other Books by Don Rich:

- GhostWRITER

Here's A Tropical Authors Novella by Deborah Brown, Nicholas Harvey, and Don Rich:

- **Priceless**

Go to my website at www.DonRichBooks.com for more information about joining my **Reader's Group**! And you can follow me on Facebook at: https://www.facebook.com/DonRichBooks

I'm also a member of TropicalAuthors.com, where you can find my latest books and those by dozens of my coastal writer friends!

www.ingramcontent.com/pod-product-compliance
Lightning Source LLC
Chambersburg PA
CBHW070356200726
48294CB00003B/934

9781959126270